CONTENTS

Editor's Preface

This book was my idea, but I had help along the way. Beatrice Behan was always enthusiastic, helpful and courteous; she made our collaboration a pleasure for me. Colbert Kearney wrote an excellent book. Rory Furlong, Edward Mikhail and Christopher Logue answered my letters and my questions.

I had help too from the staffs of the National Library in Dublin and the Periodicals Department of the British Museum and from Nóra de Brún and the staff of the library of University College, Cork.

Michael O'Brien was the good publisher; he trusted his instincts. Jean Barry typed the manuscript. Alison helped at the British Museum and Loudon first took me to The White Horse.

Introduction

Brendan Behan was born, in Dublin in 1923, into an Irish Republican family and he soon found the household's politics to be his own. In 1940 he began almost two years' detention in Borstal in England for 'complicity in acts of terrorism'. When he was arrested, he made this statement: 'My name is Brendan Behan. I came over here to fight for the Irish Workers' and Small Farmers' Republic, for a full and free life, for my fellow countrymen, North and South, and for the removal of the baneful influence of British Imperialism from Irish affairs. God save Ireland.' He was sixteen years old.

Two years later, he began five years of his prison sentence for shooting at a detective during an I.R.A. commemorative ceremony in Dublin. Many thought him lucky to escape hanging for this act. Instead he was sentenced to fourteen years' penal servitude and released under a general amnesty. In 1947 he was arrested again, this time in Manchester, 'having helped in the escape of an I.R.A. prisoner,' and he was sentenced to four months' imprisonment.

Behan seems to have appreciated his terms of confinement – he considered them his 'university' – and from the first of them he gleaned the material for his best-selling autobiography, *Borstal Boy*, and from the second and third, material for plays and stories and even the language itself for the poems and the play he wrote in Irish. Detained in the Curragh, he studied the Irish language and literature under Seán Ó Briain and Máirtín Ó Cadhain and began to conceive of the possibility of rebuilding a native Irish culture. The play, *An Giall*, was later transformed into *The Hostage*.

Perhaps there was something predictable about the course of events of his early life. One of the titles considered for his memoir of Borstal, 'Bridewell Revisited,' has about it an air of inevitability as well as of wit. The excellence of his writing could not have been foretold. But Behan had two exceptional gifts – as writer and as showman. Tragically his prowess for one would ultimately destroy the talent he'd begun to question for the other.

Writing in Irish afforded a way for Behan to realise his literary and political aspirations. In 1946 he published his first poem in *Comhar*; he had published juvenilia in *The Wolfe Tone Weekly*, *The United Irishman*, *Fianna: The Voice of Young Ireland* and other radical journals. This poem, *Filleadh Mhic Eachaidh*, a eulogy for Seán McCaughey, an I.R.A. officer who died on hunger-strike in Portlaoise, was later incorporated into *An Giall*.

In the next few years he published other poems in *Comhar*, *Envoy* and *Feasta*, and he was the youngest contributor to Seán Ó Tuama's *Nuabhéarsaíocht* (1950).

By the early 1950 s he was writing in English again and he published short prose pieces in various magazines in Paris. In *My Life with Brendan*, his widow Beatrice recalls, 'Brendan had talked to me at great length about Paris. Like James Joyce he had spent penniless years there, and he had written pornography to survive . . .' A detective story, *The Scarperer*, by 'Emmet Street' was serialised in *The Irish Times* in 1953. In 1955 he married Beatrice Salkeld.

Nineteen fifty-four was the turning point in Behan's career. It was the year in which *The Quare Fellow* was first produced by the Pike Theatre in Dublin. Two years later this play was accepted by the Theatre Royal in London. In 1958 *The Hostage* was first produced and *Borstal Boy* was published. Brendan Behan had quickly become an international celebrity, the darling of critics and the popular media. The limelight proved too much a distraction from the completion of further serious work. Plays and prose were left unfinished, ideas and promises unfulfilled. *After the Wake* is a book of uncollected and unpublished short prose pieces. It includes work of acknowledged excellence, 'The Confirmation Suit' and 'A Woman of No Standing'; of sombre detail, 'The Execution'; and of lively autobiography, 'I Become a Borstal Boy'. The unpublished pieces – and they include a short story called 'The Last of Mrs Murphy' and the opening section, all that exists, of an unfinished novel, 'The Catacombs' – are infused with compassion, wit and perceptive comment. The eponymous story, 'After the Wake,' is arguably the author's finest. It displays a degree of feeling that is honestly, humanely and courageously reported.

The selection contains all the hallmarks of the author's talent – an ability to bring characters to life quickly and unforgettably, a sharp ear for dialogue and dialect, and a natural vocation for story-telling.

His pervasive themes are rampant – the obsession with nuances of class and social structures, the inclination towards insurrection and rebellion, and the over-riding sense of moral justice. Grim situations are relieved by clemency and humour. Above all, the delicacy and holiness of human tenderness and sympathy is depicted vividly against usually unsympathetic backdrops.

The first of these stories, 'The Last of Mrs Murphy,' was submitted to Radio Éireann from the Behan home-place in Crumlin in the early '50s. The script was marked for the attention of Francis MacManus or Mervyn Wall, and Mr. Wall thinks it was broadcast as part of a series of talks Brendan Behan gave around that time. It is very much a 'Dublin' story, the characters are easily recognisable as fictional neighbours of those in 'The Confirmation Suit'. It is a story about fellowship with a surprising and spirited twist.

'I Become a Borstal Boy,' prototype of *Borstal Boy*, was accepted by Seán Ó Faoláin for publication in *The Bell* in June, 1942, sixteen years before the appearance of the extended – and altered – memoir. It tells of events after the author's first arrest and shows a conflict of emotions between the narrator's personal responses and the expected stance of one cast in his position for the 'Cause'.

This conflict is highlighted in 'The Execution' which has only been published before in a limited edition (Liffey Press, Dublin, 1978) and which I have transcribed from the author's manuscript. In his handwriting all the b's are capital B's, there are commas around almost every phrase, and almost every sentence is a separate paragraph. I have made certain modifications. 'The Execution' owes much to Frank O'Connor's story, 'Guests of the Nation,' though it is shorter and less polished. The implication of the job in hand, its human seriousness, is conveyed in one sentence: 'I never liked him much before but I felt sorry for him and sorrier for his people.' The final act exposes man's confusion in political deed and fervour.

'A Woman of No Standing' was published in *Envoy* in Dublin in 1950 and seven years later as 'That Woman' in a fashion magazine, *Creation*. The woman in question does not appear until the final paragraphs and, even then, she does not speak. Nonetheless she is the most memorable character in the story. Here Behan anticipates the success of *The Quare Fellow* whose central figure never appears on stage and who is also talked about and judged by others.

'The Confirmation Suit' is widely known. It was first published in *The Standard* in 1953 and was, with 'A Woman of No Standing,' featured in *Brendan Behan's Island*, a compilation of sketches and transcripts of recordings made, it seems, to honour a publishing contract. The most important aspect of this story is tone. Behan was able to *write* stories as a master would *tell* them. This one is both moving and funny, even if some of the jokes are dated – for instance, the woman who took a bath each year *whether she was dirty or not*. Perhaps these jokes were less familiar thirty years ago. Isn't Shakespeare the man who uses all the clichés?

'After the Wake' was published in *Points* in Paris in 1950. Could this be the 'pornography' to which Behan referred? Could his epithet be part of a shyness

13

or self-protection from subject matter which was still taboo thirty years ago? Whatever, the story treats delicately the intimacies of marriage and friendship. It is a mature and honest study of grief and solace.

The fourteen articles included here under the title, 'The Same Again, Please,' were first published in *The Irish Press* for which Behan wrote a regular column between February 1954 and April 1956. Five of them were included in *Hold Your Hour and Have Another.*

Occasionally these articles are literary – they mention Tolstoy, Raftery, Forrest Reid and the background of *The Playboy of the Western World*, but more often they ramble on about travels in Ireland and trips to the 'Continong', about Partition, Nationalism, the state of the Irish language and about Nelson's Pillar, who'll win the Derby, the time of the first 'talkie,' and Genockey's motor-car.

They're laced with songs and puns and jokes, with old Dublin sayings ('Isn't the day very changeable: you wouldn't know what to pawn'), and with tall tales. They feature characters he's used before, the cast of Jimmy-the-Sports' and the Markets' bar (Mrs. Brennan, Crippen and Maria Concepta), as well as members of his own family.

'See now, what I brought you,' he boasts in one. The comic situations, the quick, good-natured dialogue, might have found their place easily in one of his plays.

Sometimes these articles stop and start in mid-air. In one he writes simply and suddenly, 'A change is as good as a rest,' and then he begins another story. Another ends, out of the blue, 'To cause a diversion, I asked them what they were having.' In another he asides, 'I was reared a pet, God love me.' Certainly.

'The Catacombs' has never been published before. Like most of these pieces it is uneven and unfinished, and like them it is animated and engaging. It is filled with memorable characters – Uncle Hymie, Stinking Fish and the author himself, for this time there is no attempt to disguise the identity of the chief protagonist. 'You're welcome, Brendan Behan,' says Mrs Bolívar. This fragment has the stamp of autobiography more than of fiction, and in it nothing is sacred. It begins, 'There was a party to celebrate Deirdre's return from her abortion in Bristol,' and it proceeds to mock all that is sacred in Irish society, religion, politics and ethics. It stops and starts and digresses and is held together ultimately only by the presence and personality of the author.

That author wrote, reflecting on the plaque outside the Chelsea Hotel in New York City, 'However, the Chelsea Hotel respects him (Dylan Thomas) as a great artist, and I would hope that Mr. Bard, the proprietor, and his son Stanley, who has a beautiful baby daughter, would leave some space on their plaque for myself. I am not humble enough to say that I do not deserve one (sic), but I hope it does not come too soon, because of all the names on the plaque, as far as I know, James T. Farrell is the only one that's alive and kicking very much.'

By this time, Dublin's darling boy had become the whole world's roaring fellow. His death, at the age of 41, was a terrible waste as the last years of his life had been. *After the Wake* is part of an attempt to revert the spotlight from the exhibitionism and tragedy of those years to Brendan Behan's enduring literary achievement. It is also a delightful windfall.

Peter Fallon Loughcrew, Winter 1980

The Last of Mrs. Murphy

Over Mrs. Murphy's bed hung a picture of a person wearing a red jacket and a white head. When I was small I thought it was a picture of herself, but she laughed one day and said no, that it was Pope Leo. Whether this was a man or a woman I was not sure, for his red cloak was like Mrs. Murphy's and so was his white head.

The day I was five, Mrs. Murphy said we must go over to Jimmy the Sports for a quick one, the day that was in it.

'While I'm putting on me clothes, you can be giving the cat her bit of burgoo*.'

I got up the saucerful of porridge and put the milk on it, and called under the bed, 'Minnie Murphy, come out from that old shoe-box at once, and eat your breakfast'.

'Before *he* eats it,' muttered Mrs. Murphy to herself putting a skirt on over her head.

I was caught once, sitting the far side of a plateful of lights* with the cat, but that was a long time ago, when I was only three: we eating, share and share alike.

We got out of the parlour all right, and into the hall. Someone had left a pram in it and Mrs. Murphy gave it a blessing when she nearly fell over it. She supported herself going round it, and opened the hall-door. Going down the steps into the street, she rested her hand on my head. I didn't mind for she was very light, and it was easy for her to reach me, though I was not that tall, for she was bent nearly double since the winter.

Half-way up the street, she sat on the steps of 16 and said I was to run on up to the corner for a quarter ounce of white snuff.

I had to wait my turn in the shop. There were women in front of me.

'I says to myself when I seen her,' says one woman, 'the dead arose and appeared to many.'

'It's all very fine and large,' says the other old one, 'but I've had her in the Society since before the war. If she dropped dead this minute, God between her and all harm, I'd still be losing money. When she got over the Spanish 'flu, and was missed be the Tans* on Bloody Sunday, I said it was only throwing good money after bad, and I'd cut me losses and let the policy lapse, for nothing less than an Act of God or a hand grenade could make a dent in her.'

'Ah sure, what nicer am I? And we're not the only ones. There's more money invested in old Murphy nor the G.S.R.*'

The shopman looked over the counter at me, 'Well, me little man?'

'A quarter ounce of white snuff.'

The women nudged each other, 'And how's poor Mrs. Murphy today, a mhic*?'

'She's powerful.'

'God bless her and spare the poor old creature.'

'Barring the humane-killer,' muttered the other old one, and they went out.

17

In the pub she sat in the corner and ordered a bottle of stout for herself and a dandy glass of porter for me.

'An orange or something would be better for the child,' said Jimmy the Sports.

'The drop of gargle will do him good,' said Mrs. Murphy, 'it's only a little birthday celebration.'

'You must be the hundred,' said Jimmy the Sports.

'I'm not,' said old Murphy, 'nor nothing like it. I was born in the year eighteen hundred and thirty-seven.'

'You'd remember the famine then,' said Jimmy the Sports.

'We were respectable people round this street and didn't go in for famines. All shut hall-doors that time. Down in Monto* they had the famine. They didn't do a stroke of work for months only unloading the stuff off of the boats. The people that brought it over didn't mind. It was for the hungry Irish, and it saved them the trouble of going any further with it. They had the life of Riley down on the quay, while it lasted.'

Jimmy the Sports ground his teeth and looked as if he might cry. 'God forgive you, and you an old woman. My poor mother fell from her own dead mother's arms outside Loughrea workhouse.'

Mrs. Murphy took a pinch of snuff. 'Well, we all have our troubles. If it's not an ear, it's an elbow. What about the gargle?'

Jimmy the Sports put them up and she paid him. 'Sorrow sign of famine on you anyway, Jimmy. The land for the people,' she muttered to herself, 'will you ever forget that?'

We spent a bit of time in Jimmy the Sports and

then went back down the street. I walked in front for her to lean on my head, slow and in time with her. The pram was still in the hall, and she muttered a few curses getting round it, but the baby from the back drawing-room was in it this time, and she leant a minute on the side looking in at him.

'What's this the name of that crowd that owns this child is?'

'It's Rochfords' baby,' said I. 'Out of upstairs. He's only new out of the Roto* this week.'

'How do you know he's out of the Roto?'

'I heard my mother and them saying it. That's where all babies are from. They have pictures there too.'

She waved her hand. 'Shut up a minute, can't you?' She put her hand to her forehead. 'That'd be Dan Rochford's son's child, or his child maybe.' She fumbled in her handbag. 'I've two thrupenny bits. Here, take one of these in your hand. It has to be silver. Put it in the baby's hand and say what I say: "Hold your hansel, long life and the height of good luck to you." Come on.'

I tried to speak but the tears were choking me. I thought she would give me one of the thrupenny bits anyway. It was like a blow in the face to me, and I'd done nothing on her but walked nice and easy down the street when she leaned on my head, and went over and got the snuff.

She looked down at me, and I put the thrupenny bit into the pram, and turned my heart, and – cheeks and eyes all full of tears – ran through the hall and out into the street.

My mother only laughed and said it didn't mean that Mrs. Murphy fancied the baby more than she did

19

me. It could have been any new baby. It was the thing to do, and I a big fellow that had run out of two schools to be jealous of a little baby that couldn't even talk.

She brought me into Mrs. Murphy, and the two of them talked and laughed about it while I didn't look at them but sat in the corner playing with Minnie Murphy who, if she was vicious enough to scrawb you if she thought she'd get away with it, didn't make you feel such a fool. When my mother went I wanted to go too but my mother said Mrs. Murphy was sick and I could mind her till she came back.

Mrs. Murphy called me to the bedside and gave me a pinch of snuff, and had one herself, and the new baby went out of our heads.

The doctor came and said she'd have to go to the Refuge of the Dying. He told her that years ago.

Mrs. Murphy didn't know whether she'd go or not. I hoped she would. I heard them talk about it before and knew you went in a cab, miles over the city and to the southside. I was always afraid that they might have got me into another school before she'd go for, no matter how well you run out of them or kick the legs of the teacher, you have to go sometime.

She said she'd go and my granny said that she'd order a cab from the Roto to be there in the morning.

We all got into the cab. Mrs. Murphy was all wrapped up in blankets. She didn't lean on my head, but was helped by the jarvey, and off we went.

Going past a pub on the corner of Eccles Street, she said she didn't like to pass it, for old times' sake. My granny and Long Byrne and Lizzie MacCann all said they'd be the better of a rozziner*. And the jarvey came in with the rest of us. On the banks of

20

the other canal we went in and had another couple. We stopped there for a long time and my granny told the jarvey she'd make it up to him.

Glasses of malt she ordered, and Mrs. Murphy called on Long Byrne for a bar of a song.

The man in the pub said that it wasn't a singing house, but Mrs. Murphy said she was going into the Refuge and it was a kind of a wake.

So Long Byrne sang, 'When the Cock, Cock Robin, comes hop, hop, hoppin' along,' and *On Mother Kelly's Doorstep*, and for an hour it was great and you'd wish it could go on forever, but we had to go or the Refuge would be shut.

We left in Mrs. Murphy and waited in the hall. Long Byrne said you get the smell of death in it.

'It's the wax on the floors,' said my granny.

'It's a very hard-featured class of a smell, whatever it is,' said Lizzie MacCann.

'We'll never see her again now, till we come up to collect her in the box,' said Long Byrne.

'For God's sake, whisht up out of that, you,' said my granny, 'people's not bad enough.' She fumbled with her handkerchief.

'All the same, Christina,' said Lizzie MacCann, 'you'd feel bad about leaving the poor devil in a place like this.'

The jarvey was trying to smoke without being caught. 'It's a very holy place,' he said, but not looking too sure about it.

'Maybe it's that we're not that holy ourselves,' said Lizzie MacCann. 'We might sooner die medium holy, like.'

'It's not the kind of place I'd like to leave a neighbour or a neighbour's child,' said Long Byrne.

21

'Oh, whisht your mouth,' said my granny, 'you'd make me feel like an . . . an informer or something. We only do the best we can.'

A very severe looking lady in a white coat came out and stood in front of us. The jarvey stuck the pipe in his pocket and straightened his cap.

'Whars in charge of the peeshent?' she says in a very severe tongue.

My granny stood up as well as she could. 'I am, with these other women here. She's a neighbour of ours.'

'There are no admissions here after five o'clock. The patient arrived here in an intoxicated condition.'

'She means poor old Murphy was drunk,' says Long Byrne.

'The poor old creature had only about six halves, the couple of glasses of malt we had to finish up, and the few bottles we had over in Eccles Street,' said Lizzie MacCann, counting on her fingers, 'God forgive them that'd tell a lie of an old woman, that she was the worse for drink.'

'And I get a distinct smell of whiskey here in this very hall,' said the woman in the white coat.

'How well you'd know it from the smell of gin, rum or brandy,' said Long Byrne, 'Ah well, I suppose practice makes perfect.'

The woman in the white coat's face got that severe that if she fell on it she'd have cut herself.

'Out,' she put up her hand, pointing to the door, 'Out, at once.'

There was a shuffling in the back of the hall, and Mrs. Murphy came out, supported by two nurses.

'I wouldn't stop where my friends aren't welcome,' said Mrs. Murphy.

'Come on so,' says my granny.

When they got back to Jimmy the Sports, they had a few and brought some more over to Mrs. Murphy's while they put her to bed.

Long Byrne said herself and Lizzie MacCann would look after her between them.

My granny liked laziness better than she did money and said she'd bunce in a half a bar* towards their trouble.

'And it won't break you,' says Long Byrne, 'damn it all, she's not Methuselah.'

I Become a Borstal Boy

1

I awoke on the morning of the 7th February, 1940, with a feeling of despondency. I'd had a restless night and fell asleep only to be awakened an hour later by the bell that roused myself and 1,253 other prisoners in Walton Jail.

As I awoke the thought that had lain heavily with me through the night realised itself into words – *If they carry it out* . . . Just then I heard the shout 'Right, all doors open. Slop out.' . . . *they will die in two and a quarter hours.*

Then another thought followed into my mind, 'I might go down to Assizes to-day'. But I had said that every day since January 29, when I had been informed at the Committal Court that commission day for Liverpool Winter Assizes Court was six weeks off.

I rose and washed myself and settled myself to wait for the rattling of keys and opening of doors that would indicate that my breakfast was on its way. After breakfast I heard the call, 'Right, R.C's. Parade for Ash Wednesday Service,' and when the other Catholic juvenile offenders of C wing had been marched away to chapel my cell door was opened and I was escorted there in solitary state. I went to my

24

usual place between Ned, a Royal Engineer from Carlow awaiting trial for housebreaking, and Gerry, a Monaghan lad of Republican ideas and of many convictions. A whispered conversation ensued.

'Brendan,' Gerry whispered, 'they died two minutes ago.'

Down the long rows of brown-clad Remands and in the convicted pews where the blue uniform of the Borstal Boys contrasted with the grey slops of the Penal Servitudes one could see on every Irish face the imprint of the tragedy that had been enacted that morning in another prison and that was to every Irishman present a personal sorrow. Ned and Gerry nodded to me. 'O.K., Brendan, say the word.'

I stood up in my pew and raised my hand in the signal we had agreed upon the previous Sunday.

'Irishmen, attention!'

A rigid silence gripped the chapel. The warders stood bewildered. No doubt many of them thought it was a special ceremony of the Church in which the congregation took part. One young warder fingered his baton nervously.

'Irishmen, attention!'

Ned and Gerry were already on their feet.

'We will recite the *De Profundis* for the repose of the souls of our countrymen who gave their lives for Ireland this morning in Birmingham Jail.'

Gerry (who knew it) began. 'Out of the depths have I cried to thee, O Lord . . . ' Back down the serried rows came the response, 'Lord hear my voice'. An old Corkman serving seven years for manslaughter was standing in the back rows reserved for elderly Preventative Detentions. In front of him was a big Mayo lad awaiting transfer to Parkhurst or

Dartmoor. 'And let my cry come unto thee...'

Suddenly the Principal Officer appeared to regain his composure. He shouted orders. 'Remove Lawlor and Behan to their cells. Sit down the rest of you. Damn you! Silence!'

Soon I was struggling as two warders grabbed me. Ned, the big Carlow soldier, was fighting madly. Gerry's head went down amid the impact of batons. The old Corkman I last saw as they were removing him, a scarlet gash showing vividly against his white hair. Raising my head I saw a baton poised ready to strike. I crouched, tensing myself for the blow, but it never came: the P.O's voice cut in clear above the din. 'Don't strike Behan! He's for court to-day.'

I was removed to my cell and told that I was damned lucky that I was being discharged that day as otherwise I would have been reported to the Governor with the others and have got No. 1 (bread and water) 'to cool me off'.

2

Some hours later my door was opened and I heard the 'away' call: 'Right, two away for Liverpool Assizes.' I was one; the other was an alleged murderer whose trial was reaching its concluding stages. I was taken alone, however, to the reception room. There I saw six men standing in line and a seventh standing alone by the desk. He must be the alleged murderer. He smiled pleasantly and wished me 'Good morning'.

I was motioned into one of a row of cubicles and told to undress and have a bath. Having bathed I returned to my cubicle and dressed. I had been wearing prison clothes, as my own had been removed for examination and analysis by Home Office experts.

With what a thrill of pleasure I now put my hands in my trousers pockets! I was next called out to sign for the money and sundries that I had had in my possession when arrested.

'It's a waste of time with you, Paddy, doing all this bloody signing. We all know damn well you'll be back to start your twenty years!'

The warder winked at one of the escort.

'What d'you reckon you'll get, Paddy? 'Anged, drawn and quartered, or just plain 'anging?'

'Benefit of the Probation Act and ten shillings out of the Poor Box to mend my boots,' I replied.

'Yes, if you can slip that stuff over on old Mr. Justice Who-is-it, all about you bein' only sixteen years of age and so on! What is your age, Paddy — straight-up — between what's present like.'

'I was born the ninth of February, nineteen twenty-three.'

'Yes? I bet you was sixteen when Charley Peace was president of the Everton Valley Band of 'Ope. Oh well! Argue it out between yourself and Mr. Justice Who-is-it.'

And I stood aside.

'Here's the other one for Assizes, Jack!' shouted the second escort. 'O.K., Crippen! Come along.' We went along. Instead of going in the Black Maria we travelled to the city in a small police car. I took stock of my companion and thought that despite the ordeal of a four days' murder trial he appeared extraordinarily calm. He inquired where I was from and seemed surprised when I told him the nature of my offence. I was wondering in what form to put my own question, for it seemed rude to ask 'Who did you kill?' At last I found a more delicate formula. 'Who was the deceased concerned with your case?'

'Oh!' he answered, 'my wife was found about three months ago with her head battered in,' quite as if it happened by act of God. 'As we had quarrelled some days before it was not unnatural for the authorities to charge me. But, of course, I shall be acquitted.'

He spoke with such evident sincerity that when I read later an account of his execution I wondered if he had been guilty after all.

My cell at George's Hall was quite unlike those I had known in either prison or police-station. It had a barred door similar to the prison scenes in an American film. On the walls were the usual inscriptions. 'J.S. stole a lady's watch to keep it safe. 3 years P.S. 15-4-35.' In addition were inscriptions by Irishmen who had been sentenced at the previous Assizes. 'We ask no quarter – we seek no compromise. Stephen Casey.' Steve had been acquitted and was now home in his native Meath. 'Jim Flynn, 5 years P.S. Dublin Brigade.' Jim was a lad from Ringsend and had been a particular friend of mine. He was in Maidstone. 'Jerry Robinson. Operations Officer. South Wales. 15 years.' They had dealt with him rather severely, probably on account of his nationality: he was an Englishman.

I scratched my own inscription, a quotation from Pearse: 'We cannot be beaten because the cause we serve enshrines the soul of Ireland.' Under it I wrote my name and left a space for my sentence. The P.O. brought some coffee and bully-beef sandwiches. The alleged murderer had his food sent in by relatives. He asked me if I would like some banana sandwiches.

'Take the lot, son, It'll be a long time before you'll get the taste of skilly* out of your mouth.'

Amid a fanfare of trumpets the judge entered and seated himself. Then the clerk, magnificently arrayed in what appeared to be a red hunting jacket, began the list of alleged offences that constituted the bone of contention between the King and myself. I refused to plead and the prosecuting counsel, dressed in his officer's uniform, began his case. He spoke quite without passion, called his witnesses and in about two hours the case was nearly settled. I had expected a jury of twelve, but could only count eight, including three women. I wondered if any of them were annoyed with me for upsetting the routine of a shop or office. A young man of about eighteen sitting beside the judge smiled and winked at me in a comradely fashion. When the jury had returned their verdict, which they did without retiring, the Judge asked if I had anything to say before he passed sentence. I proceeded to speak and he interrupted me and told me that what I was saying wasn't likely to induce him to give me a light sentence. However, I had learnt that speech off by heart and thought it rather good and I did not intend to be sentenced without getting the worth of my money, so I told him that if it was all the same to him I would prefer to continue. When I had concluded he began himself by saying that he felt that the laws regarding the sentencing of juvenile offenders were inadequate to deal with a case like this. He made a fine speech in which he showed an acquaintance with Synge and concluded by saying that unfortunately the aforesaid laws regarding juvenile offenders did not allow him to give me the fourteen years' penal servitude which he remarked (entirely without malice) I deserved.

The only sentence he could give me there was three years' Borstal detention.

As I passed down my murderer friend was on his way to the dock. I shook hands with him and wished him luck. He smiled confidently, waved his hands and shouted 'Good-bye.' 'I hope so,' I murmured, 'for your sake.' Two and a half hours later he was removed prostrate from the dock and left in a cell next door to me. On the return journey we spoke little and even the escort conversed in subdued tones. It was like going to a funeral. As we parted finally he smiled wanly as he looked me straight in the face. 'Good luck, Paddy.'

'Right, one away Borstal landing Y.P. wing,' and in a softer tone: 'one away to D 2 14.' (The number of the condemned cell.)

As I lay in bed I calculated, as hundreds must have done in the same place, 'How soon will I get out?' I worked it out that with a bit of remission I would be released in January, 1942. I settled down for sleep. Somewhere on Merseyside a church bell rang out. It was nine o'clock . . . .

The Execution

We got Ellis into the car fairly easily – we told him we were shifting him to a new house.

God forgive me, I told the poor devil mock-confidentially that I had it from a good source that the Army Council had decided against execution and that the Battalion Staff was having him shifted to a new house because the one we were leaving had become unsafe.

We drove out to the southern outskirts of the city and when we reached a *bona fide*, Kit, who was driving, suggested a drink. We all more or less welcomed it, even Gerry Dolan (and he being a T.T. disapproved of Army men drinking whether on a job or not). Now he was on the job I don't think Gerry fancied it much.

We went in, Ellis between Kit and myself. The poor devil wouldn't have run if we'd let him. He was telling me how it wasn't his fault giving the dump away. He had never been picked up before and the cells had got in on him. Smiling contentedly to himself he was, and saying that maybe the boys wouldn't think too badly of him when he took his tar and feathering like a man. Real wistfully he said to me, 'I'd sooner get an awful beating than a tar and feathering because that'd be a terrible disgrace, my

31

old man being a '16 man an' all.' God help him. My
father was a Dublin Fusilier in 1916, but that's the
way.

I squeezed his arm in a friendly way. I'd never liked
him much before but I felt sorry for him and sorrier
for his people. He had been fond of boasting about
the Fenian tradition of his family. Still, we couldn't
let people give away dumps on us or there'd soon be
no respect for the Army.

We entered the snug.

I'd my hand through the pocket of my mac and on
my skit. It was a Police Positive .38 in a slip-holster, a
nice small skit.

Gerry Dolan, I knew, had either a Lüger, Para-
bellum, Walther or a Browning. They were the only
automatics in the company dump, except a few Colt-
autos and a 9mm Peter that was too big to lug around.
And Gerry dearly loved automatics, especially ones
with queer names. I never saw the day he'd be
satisfied with a Smith or Webley.

You can sometimes judge a fellow by his taste in
skits.

Now Kit, I could swear, would be carrying a Colt-
auto. He liked a Smith but held that it was bulky for
work like this. Although he didn't love automatics as
a rule, he'd a *grá** for the Colt. Mainly, I think,
because when he went round checking dumps with
the Batt. Q/M he could pinch a few rounds of
Thompson stuff to bang off in it. A wild lad Kit, but
dependable. A bit of a boozer. He used drink with
Mickey Horgan and Connie.

For all that I'd nearly had them dismissed for using
Army stuff on an unofficial job, I thought the three of

them the best suited of the five of us in tonight's work. Connie and Mickey would be carrying short Webleys.

I ordered drinks – four pints, a mineral for Dolan and a glass of whiskey for Ellis. They give a condemned man a glass of rum and a cigarette in France. I wished Ellis had asked for a bottle of stout. Connie, Kit and Mickey were drinking abstractedly. The frothy rings on their glasses were equi-distant.

I wasn't used to drink and was sorry I hadn't ordered an ale, a pint seemed even more unmanageable tonight.

Ellis knocked back his whiskey and asked what we were having. I didn't want to stop there all night and said we'd better be going. I was surprised when Gerry Dolan said it was his round. He ordered three pints, ale for me, and two whiskeys. His face reddened when I looked at him.

When we got in the car again Ellis's spirits seemed even further improved, the liquor I supposed. He offered me a cigarette and struck a match; his face was very young looking.

About three miles further was the spot. It would be my job to tell them to get out of the car. Ellis would see the loneliness of it. There wasn't a house in sight of it. It didn't seem so easy a thing now.

It was a frosty night and my legs were getting a bit cramped. I hoped Ellis wouldn't start crying or anything. I'd sooner he put up a fight. It would be easier to let him have it.

'Let him have it,' 'plugging him,' 'knocking him off'. It's small wonder people are shy of describing the deed properly. We were going to kill him.

With a jolt the car pulled up.

Kit turned round from the wheel, 'O.K. to get out lads?' No one answered.

It seemed a hundred years before I nudged Ellis. 'Come on, get out.'

A death sentence – that's what it was – and I saw that he realised it.

I flashed my torch on him. His jaw dropped but he obeyed.

We brought him in about fifteen yards off the road. He didn't murmur.

Gerry Dolan shook my arm, his face was white in the moonlight. His lips grinned as he struggled to find words; he said something about an Act of Contrition. His fancy 9mm shook in his hand. I nodded.

All was in readiness. The handles of the shovels were dimly outlined behind a bush. We stood at the spot. Kit was lighting a cigarette, his hand cupping the flame.

Ellis looked round him, just a little wildly. 'Not yet, lads,' he moaned. He began to cry not wildly but softly, the way a child cries. The tears streamed down his cheeks.

Kit Whelan patted his shoulder.

I wondered what to say to comfort him.

I could hardly tell him it was quite painless, we'd be sure to get the heart. After all he wasn't having a tooth out.

He knelt down and began to pray.

We knelt down with him.

I tried to pray for his soul. I couldn't. It seemed awful to think of souls just then.

We arose and he bent his head close to his body,

as if to avoid a blow.

I raised my revolver close to his head, not too close.

If I put it against his head maybe the muzzle would get blood on it, blood and hair, hair with Brillantine on it.

The five guns were levelled at him.

I cocked mine and pressed slowly on the trigger. It seemed to take all my strength.

There was a deafening roar and he pitched wildly forward. I heard more shots and he lay still.

As if in a dream I saw Connie eject the empty shells. Kit was picking them off the ground from his Auto.

'Finished, the poor divil,' he murmured.

We put him in the grave. He felt quite warm. I told the lads to be careful not to get bloodstains on their clothes. We began to shovel in earth. I moved a big stone off my shovel – it might smash in his face.

The Confirmation Suit

For weeks it was nothing but simony and sacrilege, and the sins crying to heaven for vengeance, the big green Catechism in our hands, walking home along the North Circular Road. And after tea, at the back of the brewery wall, with a butt too to help our wits, what is a pure spirit, and don't kill that, Billser has to get a drag out of it yet, what do I mean by apostate, and hell and heaven and despair and presumption and hope. The big fellows, who were now thirteen and the veterans of last year's Confirmation, frightened us, and said the Bishop would fire us out of the Chapel if we didn't answer his questions, and we'd be left wandering around the streets, in a new suit and top-coat with nothing to show for it, all dressed up and nowhere to go. The big people said not to mind them; they were only getting it up for us, jealous because they were over their Confirmation, and could never make it again. At school we were in a special room to ourselves, for the last few days, and went round, a special class of people. There were worrying times too, that the Bishop would light on you, and you wouldn't be able to answer his questions. Or you might hear the women complaining about the price of boys' clothes.

'Twenty-two and sixpence for tweed, I'd expect a

share in the shop for that. I've a good mind to let him go in jersey and pants for that.'

'Quite right, ma'am', says one to another, backing one another up, 'I always say what matter if they are good and pure'. What had that got to do with it, if you had to go into the Chapel in a jersey and pants, and every other kid in a new suit, kid gloves and tan shoes and a *scoil** cap. The Cowan brothers were terrified. They were twins, and twelve years old, and every old one in the street seemed to be wishing a jersey and pants on them, and saying their poor mother couldn't be expected to do for two in the one year, and she ought to go down to Sister Monica and tell her to put one back. If it came to that, the Cowans agreed to fight it out, at the back of the brewery wall; whoever got best, the other would be put back.

I wasn't so worried about this. My old fellow was a tradesman, and made money most of the time. Besides, my grandmother, who lived at the top of the next house, was a lady of capernosity and function. She had money and lay in bed all day, drinking porter or malt, and taking pinches of snuff, and talking to the neighbours that would call up to tell her the news of the day. She only left her bed to go down one flight of stairs and visit the lady in the back drawing room, Miss McCann.

Miss McCann worked a sewing-machine, making habits for the dead. Sometimes girls from our quarter got her to make dresses and costumes, but mostly she stuck to the habits. They were a steady line, she said, and you didn't have to be always buying patterns, for the fashions didn't change, not even from summer to winter. They were like a long brown shirt, and a hood

37

attached, that was closed over the person's face before the coffin lid was screwn down. A sort of little banner hung out of one arm, made of the same material, and four silk rosettes in each corner, and in the middle, the letters I.H.S., which mean, Miss McCann said, 'I Have Suffered'.

My grandmother and Miss McCann liked me more than any other kid they knew. I like being liked, and could only admire their taste.

My Aunt Jack, who was my father's aunt as well as mine, sometimes came down from where she lived, up near the Basin, where the water came from before they started getting it from Wicklow. My Aunt Jack said it was much better water, at that. Miss McCann said she ought to be a good judge. For Aunt Jack was funny. She didn't drink porter or malt, or take snuff, and my father said she never thought much about men either. She was also very strict about washing yourself very often. My grandmother took a bath every year, whether she was dirty or not, but she was in no way bigoted in the washing line in between times.

Aunt Jack made terrible raids on us now and again, to stop snuff and drink, and make my grandmother get up in the morning, and wash herself, and cook meals and take food with them. My grandmother was a gilder by trade, and served her time in one of the best shops in the city, and was getting a man's wages at sixteen. She liked stuff out of the pork butchers, and out of cans, but didn't like boiling potatoes, for she said she was no skivvy, and the chip man was better at it. When she was left alone it was a pleasure to eat with her. She always had cans of lovely things and spicy meat and brawn, and plenty of seasoning, fresh out of the German man's shop up the road. But after a visit from Aunt Jack, she would have to get up and wash for a week, and she would have to go and make stews and boil cabbage and pig's cheeks. Aunt Jack was very much up for sheep's heads too. They were so cheap and nourishing.

But my grandmother only tried it once. She had been a first-class gilder in Eustace Street, but never had anything to do with sheep's heads before. When she took it out of the pot, and laid it on the plate, she and I sat looking at it, in fear and trembling. It was bad enough going into the pot, but with the soup streaming from its eyes, and its big teeth clenched in a very bad temper, it would put the heart crossways in you. My grandmother asked me, in a whisper, if I ever thought sheep could look so vindictive, but that it was more like the head of an old man, and would I for God's sake take it up and throw it out of the window. The sheep kept glaring at us, but I came the far side of it, and rushed over to the window and threw it out in a flash. My grandmother had to drink a Baby Power whiskey, for she wasn't the better of herself.

Afterwards she kept what she called her stock-pot on the gas. A heap of bones and, as she said herself, any old muck that would come in handy, to have boiling there, night and day, on a glimmer. She and I ate happily of cooked ham and California pineapple and sock-eyed salmon, and the pot of good nourishing soup was always on the gas even if Aunt Jack came down the chimney, like the Holy Souls at midnight. My grandmother said she didn't begrudge the money for the gas. Not when she remembered the looks that sheep's head was giving her. And all she had to do with the stock-pot was throw in another sup of water, now and again, and a handful of old rubbish the pork butcher would send over, in the way of lights or bones. My Aunt Jack thought a lot about barley, too, so we had a package of that lying beside the gas, and threw a sprinkle in any time her foot was heard on the stairs. The stock-pot bubbled away on the gas for years after, and only when my grandmother was dead did someone notice it. They tasted it, and spat it out just as quick, and wondered what it was. Some said it was paste, and more that it was gold size, and there were other people and they maintained that it was glue. They all agreed on one thing, that it was dangerous tack to leave lying around where there might be young children, and in the heel of the reel, it went out the same window as the sheep's head.

Miss McCann told my grandmother not to mind Aunt Jack but to sleep as long as she liked in the morning. They came to an arrangement that Miss McCann would cover the landing and keep an eye out. She would call Aunt Jack in for a minute, and give the signal by banging the grate, letting on to poke the fire, and have a bit of a conversation with Aunt Jack about dresses and costumes, and hats and habits. One of these mornings, and Miss McCann delaying a fighting action, to give my grandmother time to hurl herself out of bed and into her clothes and give her face the rub of a towel, the chat between Miss McCann and Aunt Jack came to my Confirmation suit.

When I made my first Communion, my grandmother dug deep under the mattress, and myself and Aunt Jack were sent round expensive shops, and I came back with a rig that would take the sight of your eye. This time, however, Miss McCann said there wasn't much stirring in the habit line, on account of the mild winter, and she would be delighted to make the suit, if Aunt Jack would get the material. I nearly wept, for terror of what these old women would have me got up in, but I had to let on to be delighted, Miss McCann was so set on it. She asked Aunt Jack did she remember my father's Confirmation suit. He did. He said he would never forget it. They sent him out in a velvet suit, of plum colour, with a lace collar. My blood ran cold when he told me.

The stuff they got for my suit was blue serge, and that was not so bad. They got as far as the pants, and that passed off very civil. You can't do much to a boy's pants, one pair is like the next, though I had to ask them not to trouble themselves putting three little buttons on either side of the legs. The waistcoat was all right, and anyway the coat would cover it. But the coat itself, that was where Aughrim* was lost.

The lapels were little wee things, like what you'd see in pictures like Ring magazine of John L. Sullivan, or Gentleman Jim, and the buttons were the size of saucers, or within the bawl of an ass of it, and I nearly cried when I saw them being put on, and ran down to my mother, and begged her to get me any suit of a suit, even a jersey and pants, than have me set up before the people in this get-up. My mother said it was very kind of Aunt Jack and Miss McCann to go to all this trouble and expense, and I was very ungrateful not to appreciate it. My father said that Miss McCann was such a good tailor that people were dying to get into her creations, and her

41

handiwork was to be found in all the best cemeteries. He laughed himself sick at this, and said if it was good enough for him to be sent down to North William Street in plum-coloured velvet and lace, I needn't be getting the needle over a couple of big buttons and little lapels. He asked me not to forget to get up early the morning of my Confirmation, and let him see me, before he went to work: a bit of a laugh started the day well. My mother told him to give over and let me alone, and said she was sure it would be a lovely suit, and that Aunt Jack would never buy poor material, but stuff that would last forever. That nearly finished me altogether, and I ran through the hall up to the corner, fit to cry my eyes out, only I wasn't much of a hand at crying. I went more for cursing, and I cursed all belonging to me, and was hard at it on my father, and wondering why his lace collar hadn't choked him, when I remembered that it was a sin to go on like that, and I going up for Confirmation, and I had to simmer down, and live in fear of the day I'd put on that jacket.

The days passed, and I was fitted and refitted, and every old one in the house came up to look at the suit, and took a pinch of snuff, and a sup out of the jug, and wished me long life and the health to wear and tear it, and they spent that much time viewing it round, back, belly and sides, that Miss McCann hadn't time to make the overcoat, and like an answer to a prayer, I was brought down to Talbot Street, and dressed out in a dinging overcoat, belted, like a grown-up man's. And my shoes and gloves were dear and dandy, and I said to myself that there was no need to let anyone see the suit with its little lapels and big buttons. I could keep the topcoat on all day, in the chapel and going round afterwards.

The night before Confirmation day, Miss McCann handed over the suit to my mother, and kissed me, and said not to bother thanking her. She would do more than that for me, and she and my grandmother cried and had a drink on the strength of my having grown to be a big fellow, in the space of twelve years, which they didn't seem to consider a great deal of time. My father said to my mother, and I getting bathed before the fire, that since I was born Miss McCann thought the world of me. When my mother was in hospital, she took me into her place till my mother came out, and it near broke her heart to give me back.

In the morning I got up, and Mrs. Rooney in the next room shouted in to my mother that her Liam was still stalling, and not making any move to get out of it, and she thought she was cursed; Christmas or Easter, Communion or Confirmation, it would drive a body into Riddleys, which is the mad part of Grangegorman*, and she wondered she wasn't driven out of her mind, and above in the puzzle factory years ago. So she shouted again at Liam to get up and washed and dressed. And my mother shouted at me, though I was already knotting my tie, but you might as well be out of the world as out of fashion, and they kept it up like a pair of mad women, until at last Liam and I were ready and he came in to show my mother his clothes. She hanselled him a tanner which he put in his pocket and Mrs. Rooney called me in to show her my clothes. I just stood at her door, and didn't open my coat, but just grabbed the sixpence out of her hand, and ran up the stairs like the hammers of hell. She shouted at me to hold on a minute, she hadn't seen my suit, but I muttered something about it not being lucky to keep a Bishop waiting, and ran on.

The Church was crowded, boys on one side and the girls on the other, and the altar ablaze with lights and flowers, and a throne for the Bishop to sit on when he wasn't confirming. There was a cheering crowd outside, drums rolled, trumpeters from Jim Larkin's band sounded the Salute. The Bishop came in and the doors were shut. In short order I joined the queue to the rails, knelt and was whispered over, and touched on the cheek. I had my overcoat on the whole time, though it was warm, and I was in a lather of sweat waiting for the hymns and the sermon.

The lights grew brighter and I got warmer, was carried out fainting. But though I didn't mind them loosening my tie, I clenched firmly my overcoat, and nobody saw the jacket with the big buttons and the little lapels. When I went home I got into bed, and my father said I went into a sickness just as the Bishop was giving us the pledge. He said this was a master stroke and showed real presence of mind.

Sunday after Sunday, my mother fought over the suit. She said I was a liar and a hypocrite, putting it on for a few minutes every week, and running into Miss McCann's and out again, letting her think I wore it every week-end. In a passionate temper my mother said she would show me up, and tell Miss McCann, and up like a shot with her, for my mother was always slim and light on her feet as a feather, and in next door. When she came back she said nothing, but sat at the fire looking into it. I didn't really believe she would tell Miss McCann. And I put on the suit and thought I would go in and tell her I was wearing it this week-night, because I was going to the Queen's with my brothers. I ran next door and upstairs, and every step was more certain and easy that my mother hadn't told her. I ran, shoved in the door, saying: 'Miss Mc., Miss Mc., Rory and Sean and I are going to the Queen's . . .' She was bent over the sewing-machine and all I could see was the top of her old grey head, and the rest of her shaking with crying, and her arms folded under her head, on a bit of habit where she had been finishing the I.H.S. I ran down the stairs and back into our place, and my mother was sitting at the fire, sad and sorry, but saying nothing.

I needn't have worried about the suit lasting forever. Miss McCann didn't. The next winter was not so mild, and she was whipped before the year was out. At her wake people said how she was in a habit of her own making, and my father said she would look queer in anything else, seeing as she supplied the dead of the whole quarter for forty years, without one complaint from a customer.

At the funeral, I left my topcoat in the carriage and got out and walked in the spills of rain after her coffin. People said I would get my end, but I went on till we reached the graveside, and I stood in my Confirmation suit drenched to the skin. I thought this was the least I could do.

After the Wake

When he sent to tell me she was dead, I thought that
if the dead live on – which I don't believe they do –
and know the minds of the living, she'd feel angry,
not so much jealous as disgusted, certainly surprised.

For one time she had told me, quoting uncon-
sciously from a book I'd lent him, 'A woman can
always tell them – you kind of smell it on a man –
like knowing when a cat is in a room'.

We often discussed things like that – he, always a
little cultured, happy, and proud to be so broad-
minded – she, with adolescent pride in the freedom
of her married state to drink a bottle of stout and talk
about anything with her husband and her husband's
friend.

I genuinely liked them both. If I went a week
without calling up to see them, he was down the
stairs to our rooms, asking what they'd done on me,
and I can't resist being liked. When I'd go in she'd
stick a fag in my mouth and set to making tea for me.

I'd complimented them, individually and together,
on their being married to each other – and I meant it.

They were both twenty-one, tall and blond, with a
sort of English blondness.

He, as I said, had pretensions to culture and was
genuinely intelligent, but that was not the height of

his attraction for me.

Once we went out to swim in a weir below the Dublin Mountains. It was evening time and the last crowd of kids too shrimpish, small, neutral cold to take my interest – just finishing their bathe.

When they went off, we stripped and, watching him, I thought of Marlowe's lines which I can't remember properly: 'Youth with gold wet head, through water gleaming, gliding, and crowns of pearlets on his naked arms'.

I haven't remembered it at all, but only the sense of a Gaelic translation I've read.

When we came out we sat on his towel – our bare thighs touching – smoking and talking.

We talked of the inconveniences of tenement living. He said he'd hated most of all sleeping with his brothers – so had I, I'd felt their touch incestuous – but most of all he hated sleeping with a man older than himself.

He'd refused to sleep with his father which hurt the old man very much, and when a seizure took his father in the night, it left him remorseful.

'I don't mind sleeping with a little child,' he said, 'the snug way they round themselves into you – and I don't mind a young fellow my own age'.

'The like of myself,' and I laughed as if it meant nothing. It didn't apparently, to him.

'No, I wouldn't mind you, and it'd be company for me, if she went into hospital or anything,' he said.

Then he told me what she herself had told me sometime before, that there was something the matter with her, something left unattended since she was fourteen or so, and that soon she'd have to go into hospital for an operation.

47

From that night forward, I opened the campaign in jovial earnest.

The first step – to make him think it manly, ordinary to manly men, the British Navy, 'Porthole Duff', 'Navy Cake' stories of the Hitler Youth in captivity, told me by Irish soldiers on leave from guarding them; to remove the taint of 'cissiness', effeminacy, how the German Army had encouraged it in Cadet Schools, to harden the boy-officers, making their love a muscular clasp of friendship, independent of women, the British Public Schools, young Boxers I'd known (most of it about the Boxers was true), that Lord Alfred Douglas was son to the Marquess of Queensbury and a good man to use his dukes himself, Oscar Wilde throwing old 'Q' down the stairs and after him his Ballyboy attendant.

On the other front, appealing to that hope of culture – Socrates, Shakespeare, Marlow – lies, truth and half-truth.

I worked cautiously but steadily. Sometimes (on the head of a local scandal) in conversation with them both.

After I'd lent him a book about an English schoolmaster, she'd made the remark about women knowing, scenting them as she would a cat in a dark, otherwise empty room.

Quite undeliberately, I helped tangle her scents.

One night we'd been drinking together, he and I, fairly heavily up in their rooms.

I remember when he'd entered and spoken to her, he said to me: 'Your face lights up when you see her'. And why wouldn't it? Isn't a kindly welcome a warming to both faith and features?

I went over and told her what he'd said.

'And my face lights up when I see yours,' she said, smiling up at me in the charming way our women have with half-drunk men.

The following morning I was late for work with a sick head.

I thought I'd go upstairs to their rooms and see if there was a bottle of stout left that would cure me.

There wasn't, and though she was in, he was out.

I stopped a while and she gave me a cup of tea, though I'd just finished my own down below in our place.

As I was going she asked me had I fags for the day. I said I had – so as not to steal her open store, as the saying has it – and went off to work.

She, or someone, told him I'd been in and he warned me about it the next time we were together. He didn't mind (and I believed him) but people talked, etc.

From that day forward I was cast as her unfortunate admirer, my jealousy of him sweetened by my friendship for them both.

She told me again about her operation and asked me to pray for her. When I protested my unsuitability as a pleader with God, she quoted the kindly, highly heretical Irish Catholicism about the prayers of the sinner being first heard.

The night before she went into hospital we had a good few drinks – the three of us together.

We were in a singing house on the Northside and got very sob-gargled between drinking whiskey and thinking of the operation.

I sang My Mary of the Curling Hair and when we came to the Gaelic chorus, 'siúil, a ghrá' ('walk, my

49

love'), she broke down in sobbing and said how he knew as well as she that it was to her I was singing, but that he didn't mind. He said that indeed he did not, and she said how fearful she was of this operation, that maybe she'd never come out of it. She was not sorry for herself, but for him, if anything happened her and she died on him, aye, and sorry for me too, maybe more sorry, 'Because, God help you,' she said to me, 'that never knew anything better than going down town half-drunk and dirty rotten bitches taking your last farthing'.

Next day was Monday, and at four o'clock she went into the hospital. She was operated on on Thursday morning and died the same evening at about nine o'clock.

When the doctor talked about cancer, he felt consoled a little. He stopped his dry-eyed sobbing and came with me into a public-house where we met his mother and hers and made arrangements to have her brought home and waked in her own place.

She was laid out in the front room on their spare single bed which was covered in linen for the purpose. Her habit was of blue satin and we heard afterwards that some old ones considered the colour wrong – her having been neither a virgin nor a member of the Children of Mary Sodality.

The priest, a hearty man who read Chesterton and drank pints, disposed of the objection by saying that we were all Children of Mary since Christ introduced St. John to our Lady at the foot of the Cross – Son, behold thy Mother; Mother, behold Thy Son.

It is a horrible thing how quickly death and disease can work on a body.

She didn't look like herself, any more than the

brown parchment-thin shell of a mummy looks like an Egyptian warrior; worse than the mummy, for he at least is dry and clean as dust. Her poor nostrils were plugged with cotton-wool and her mouth hadn't closed properly, but showed two front teeth, like a rabbit's. All in all, she looked no better than the corpse of her granny, or any other corpse for that matter.

There was a big crowd at the wake. They shook hands with him and told him they were sorry for his trouble; then they shook hands with his and her other relatives, and with me, giving me an understanding smile and licence to mourn my pure unhappy love.

Indeed, one old one, far gone in Jameson, said she was looking down on the two of us, expecting me to help him bear up.

Another old one, drunker still, got lost in the complications of what might have happened had he died instead of her, and only brought herself up at the tableau — I marrying her and he blessing the union from on high.

At about midnight, they began drifting away to their different rooms and houses and by three o'clock there was only his mother left with us, steadily drinking.

At last she got up a little shakily on her feet and, proceeding to knock her people, said that they'd left bloody early for blood relatives, but seeing as they'd given her bloody little in life it was the three of us were best entitled to sit waking — she included me and all.

When his mother went, he told me he felt very sore and very drunk and very much in need of sleep.

He felt hardly able to undress himself.

I had to almost carry him to the big double bed in the inner room.

I first loosened his collar to relieve the flush on his smooth cheeks, took off his shoes and socks and pants and shirt, from the supply muscled thighs, the stomach flat as an altar boy's, and noted the golden smoothness of the blond hair on every part of his firm white flesh.

I went to the front room and sat by the fire till he called me.

'You must be nearly gone yourself,' he said, 'you might as well come in and get a bit of rest.'

I sat on the bed, undressing myself by the faint flickering of the candles from the front room.

I fancied her face looking up from the open coffin on the Americans who, having imported wakes from us, invented morticians themselves.

A Woman of No Standing

'And the priest turns round to me' says Ria, 'and says he: "But you don't mean to say that this person still goes down to see him?"'

'"I do, Father."'

'"And brings him cigarettes?"'

'"Not now, Father, not cigarettes, he's gone past smoking and well past it, but a drop of chicken soup, though he can't manage that either, these last few days."'

'"Well, chicken soup or cigarettes," says the priest, "what really matters is that this person continues to visit him – continues to trouble his conscience – continues as a walking occasion of sin to stand between him and heaven. These Pigeon House people must be, shall be, told straight away. They'll be informed that you, and you only, are his lawfully wedded wife, and that she is only – what she is. Anyway, this way or that, into that sanatorium she goes no more."'

'You know,' puts in Máire, when Ria had finished, 'it's a known thing and a very well-known thing, that a person cannot die while there's something not settled in his conscience. That one going to see him so, outside of the insult to Mammy here, his lawful wife, not to mind me, his only daughter, for all we're away from him since I was five – on the top of all that she was doing his soul the height of injury, not to mind holding his body in a ferment of pain, below on this earth, down in that Pigeon House.'

'But no matter,' says Ria, 'the priest wasn't long about seeing the Reverend Mother and leaving strict instructions that she wasn't to be let in any more – that she was no more his lawful wedded wife than the holy nun herself.'

'So now,' said Máire, 'if you don't go down early tomorrow you'll not see him at all, because I doubt if his struggling spirit will back away from Judgement any more, now that all is settled, and his mind at ease.'

He was still alive when I got down to the Pigeon House but she wasn't far out, because he didn't last out the night.

His face all caved in, and his hair that was once so brown and curly was matted in sweat, and God knows what colour.

Ah, you'd pity him all right, for the ruined remains of what was once the gassest* little ex-Dublin Fusilier in the street – off with the belt and who began it – Up the Toughs, Throttle the Turks, and Hell blast Gallipoli.

Ria, his wife, was the kindest woman in Ireland, and (I've heard my mother say) in her day, the best looking.

He died that night and the nun and Ria and Máire were charmed that he'd no mortal sin on his soul to detain him in torment for any longer than a few short years of harmonious torture in Purgatory.

The priest was delighted too, because, as he said: 'It's not when you die, but how you die that matters.'

54

As for the woman, no one saw her to know what she thought of it, but the priest gave strict orders that she wasn't to be let near the funeral.

The funeral was on the day after. He'd lain the night before in the mortuary chapel. They've a mortuary chapel in the Pigeon House sanatorium, nice and handy, and most soothing, I'm sure, to new patients coming in, it being close by the entrance gate.

There used to be an old scribble on the porch that said: 'Let all who enter here, leave hope behind.' But some hard chaw* had the beatings of that and wrote: 'It's only a step from Killarney to heaven – come here and take the lift – any lung, chum?'

We had a few prayers that night, but she never turned up, and I was sorry, because to tell the truth, I was curious to see her.

At the funeral next day, our cars (Ria did it in style all right, whatever lingering scald her heart might hold for him) greased off the wet Pigeon House Road, through Ringsend, and into Pearse Street, and still no sign of her. Right up the Northside, and all the way to Glasnevin, and she never appeared.

Ria had the hearse go round the block where we'd all lived years ago – happy, healthy, though riotous betimes – fighting being better than loneliness.

I thought she'd have ambushed us here, but she didn't.

I had some idea of a big car (owned by a new and tolerant admirer) sweeping into the cortège from some side street or another, or else a cab that'd slide in, a woman in rich mourning heavily veiled in its corner.

But between the Pigeon House and the grave not a

55

one came near us.

The sods were thrown in and all, and the grave-diggers well away to it when Máire spotted her.

'Mother, get the full of your eyes of that one.'

'Where, *alanna**?,' asks Ria.

'There,' said Máire, pointing towards a tree behind us. I looked towards it.

All I could see was a poor middle-aged woman, bent in haggard prayer, dressed in the cast-off hat and coat of some *flahool** old one she'd be doing a day's work for (maybe not so *flahool* either, for sometimes they'll stop a day's pay on the head of some old rag, rejected from a jumble sale).

'But I thought,' says I to Ria, 'that she'd be like – like – that she'd be dolled up to the nines – paint and powder and a fur coat maybe.'

'Fur coat how are you!,' said Ria scornfully, 'and she out scrubbing halls for me dear departed this last four years – since he took bad.'

She went off from behind her tree before we left the cemetery.

When Ria, Máire and myself got into The Brian Boru, there she was at the end of the counter.

I called two drinks and a mineral for Máire, and as soon as she heard my voice, she looked up, finished her gill of plain porter and went off.

She passed quite near us and she going out the door – her head down and a pale hunted look in her eyes.

The Catacombs

There was a party to celebrate Deirdre's return from her abortion in Bristol.

Ciarán, her brother, welcomed me, literally with open arms, when I entered the Catalonian Cabinet Room where the guests were assembled.

Even her mother, the screwy old bitch, came over with a glass of whiskey in her hand, and said, 'You're welcome, Brendan Behan.'

Bloody well, I knew why I was welcome.

It was I squared the matter for Deirdre to go over to England, and have her baby out, under the National Health Service, so to speak.

The mother was supposed to be a very good Catholic and I was a bit shocked to see the matter of fact way she accepted the situation and even put up the money for the trip and the readies* to pay the quack.

She never let on to know, of course, that there was anything amiss (no pun) and pretended to believe that Deirdre was 'going on a bit of a holiday to the other side.'

Deirdre and Ciarán's father was Irish Representative of the Catalonian Government at the time of the Spanish War and had been instrumental, it was said, in preventing the Irish Government from recognising

Franco till the whole thing was over and it didn't matter any more.

There was great pressure to recognise Franco brought on the Government by the Cardinal and Bishops of Ireland, but it was said that De Valera had some sympathy with the Catalonians and Basques, on account of having relations amongst them. It might also have been the case that he was remembering when he was President of the Irish Republic and was excommunicated by the same Bishops.

Mr. Bolívar, Ciarán's and Deirdre's father, ran a wine business in Dublin, and even when his side lost the Spanish War, his diplomatic skill stood him in good stead. He got the right side of the Bishops by presenting the Cardinal with a magnificent fifteenth century chalice which he had rescued from sacrilege. It was said that he rescued a few chalices for himself, while he was at it, and sold them to American millionaires for vast sums.

A minority of the Bishops kicked up a row over the Cardinal accepting the chalice from a former agent of the Reds, but the Cardinal fell in love with it, and blessed Mr. Bolívar, and forgave him his trespasses.

The situation got a bit more complicated after that because Franco's crowd were recognised, and his new Ambassador to Ireland dropped a gentle hint that they wouldn't mind having their chalice back. At one stage of the game, they even contemplated legal action in the Irish Courts to secure its return, and contacted Mr. Bolívar to give evidence for them. They offered him a fair sum of money for his trouble, but he said that though he was a former anarchist he could not see his way, as a Catholic, to going against the Cardinal in a law case.

His attitude in this matter even made him popular again with the Knights of Columbanus, the Catholic Freemasons, who compete with the Protestant Freemasons for contracts and sometimes combine with them to keep up prices in the shops. It was agreed by the Knights that Mr. Bolívar was a true Papist, at the back of his politics, and his anarchism was excused on the grounds that he wasn't doing it for nothing.

Mr. Bolívar's attachment to the Anarchist Republic of Catalonia had never interfered with his business of wine importing and potato exporting.

During his term as a diplomat he used to say at dinners and receptions, as reported in the newspapers, 'It is good for our two countries – Ireland needs the civilising wine and Catalonia needs the strengthening spuds. *Éire go Bráth!** I Visca Catalunya!'

Mr. Bolívar often used stage-Irish expressions from America, like 'spuds' for potatoes, because he was born in Mexico City.

His father was half-Irish, and his mother was of purely Irish descent. In many countries of South America there are large cattle-owning colonies of Irish people descended from settlers who emigrated in the 1840s and '50s from the grazing country of the Irish Midlands.

They are now an immensely wealthy group, and their eldest sons are sent home to Mullingar and Athlone and Kildare to be educated. One of them is mentioned in James Joyce's *Portrait of the Artist as a Young Man.* 'The higher line fellows began to come down along the matting in the middle of the refectory –

Paddy Rath and Jimmy Magee, and the Spaniard who was allowed to smoke cigars and the little Portuguese who wore the woolly cap.'

These South American Irish are intensely proud of their ancestry, and have a snobbish horror of Irish-Americans from the United States. They also, when in Ireland, have the strong farmer's prejudice against the Dublin and Belfast working-class, whom they regard as slum-dwellers. Though it contains, as noted above, many stage- and screen-Irishisms, their English speech is that of Counties Meath, Westmeath, Kildare and Longford.

For a time after Franco's victory, Mr. Bolívar was not permitted to do business with any part of Spain, but when things settled down, it was discovered by Franco's Embassy that as long as Mr. De Valera's party ruled the country, they must do business with Mr. Bolívar or get no spuds. For Mr. Bolívar, in his day, had been representative of the Irish Republic in South America.

In the Catalonian Cabinet Room hung his mementoes of earlier Republics. A manifesto signed by, amongst others, Señor Loyola Bolívar, on behalf of: 'Los Libertadores en la América del Sur.
La Raza Gaélica.
Los pueblos ya no podrán ser manejados como el alfil sobre el tablero. Ellos serán los únicos árbitros de sus propios destinos.'

Presidente Wilson occupied one side of the mantelpiece, and on the other side was a large and beautifully engraved Irish Republican Bond:

'República de Irlanda.
Certificado de Título.
Diez Pesos.
A..............
Yo, Éamon De Valera, Presidente de Gobierno de la República de Irlanda –' and more to the same effect I've no doubt, dated Febrero, 1921.

So, in the Irish Government, Mr. Bolívar had many friends, and devil a much good the Bishops could do the Caudillo, so long as De Valera's party was in power, and if Franco wanted Irish spuds, he had to get them through the same source that the Reds got them.

For the Fianna Fáil crowd recognised but the one true Pope, by the name of Éamon De Valera, late of 42nd St., and lesser Popes were taken notice of only in a religious way.

They would always grant his Holiness censorship of immoral publications (such as this) but a tariff or a trading quota was, as my sincere colleague the late Anton Chekhov would say, a character out of a different opera.

So, Mr. Bolívar re-opened his trade with Spain and announced to his friends of the Friends of the Spanish Republic that it would be only penalising the proletariat there by refusing to send them any spuds.

He had other interests besides wine and potatoes, and for years had a big house in the County Dublin between the mountains and the sea. He ran two cars – one of them a large Hispano-Suiza.

Though an abstemious man, the cooking of his Basque chef was famous, and his cellar was one of the best in Ireland.

'If Loyola Bolívar did not have a good sup of wine,'

said the other Dublin businessmen 'in the name of God – who would?'

Besides, the businessmen at Loyola's table were usually supposed to be on diets. They were not very strict about these diets, only for a few days after the death of one of their number, but they preferred to diet on an excess of whiskey or claret than on an excess of starch.

It was agreed on all hands that Loyola's lunches and dinners would have been worth ten times as long a journey, and out to his house trooped the businessmen who ate and drank and did deals over the cognacs till Mrs. Bolívar lost her temper one day, and from an upstairs window dropped an Ibizenco fish-weight on the head of the President of the Scottish Widows Mutual Financial Trust while he stood at the hall-door waiting for his car to drive up and thanking Mr. Bolívar for a wonderful lunch.

Mrs. Bolívar and Loyola married when he was twenty-one years old and she was a shy girl of eighteen from the plains of Kildare, living the simple, ample, and happy life, the only daughter of an Irish grazier.

Horses and cattle were the great interest of the countryside, and the devil and as much María Bolívar didn't know about them.

Her maiden name was the same as her lover's, for they were third cousins. It was in their great grand-uncle's house that they met when he was a schoolboy on holidays.

María hunted in the season and went to Dublin in August for the Horse Show, and in May for the Spring Show, and for two weeks after Christmas to see Jimmy O'Dea in the Gaiety Pantomime and to help her mother order vast quantities of clothing at the January Sales.

Twice she had been to the Continent; once to Rome for the Ordination of her favourite brother, Louis, and to Lourdes with her mother, when the old lady's health began to fail.

On both occasions they travelled straight through London on the Wagons-Lits, but stopped some days in Paris, going and coming.

London they considered a shabby receptacle for poverty-stricken Irish people and petty criminals on the run.

María could play the piano, spoke French and could speak – but not read – Spanish which she learned from her cousins on their trips home from Latin America. She was elegant, beautiful, and when amongst her own sort of people, amiable and good-humoured, whether they were servant boys or graziers.

At a harvest home, there was porter and pig's cheek, with home made-bread, and María the life and soul of the party. An artless *cailín**, she moved amongst the farmworkers and dairymaids with an easy grace, and laughed and danced and played hornpipes on the fiddle for the party.

Loyola she had known since they were children and when he asked her to marry him, it was considered on all sides an excellent match.

They were closely enough related to consolidate the wealth and lands of the *Clann** Bolívar, but not closely enough to bring them within the degrees of kindred and consanguinity forbidden by the fifth Precept of the Church.

63

So, they were married and went to Paris for her shopping – a wedding present from Loyola; to Rome for the blessing of Pope Pius XI, Achille Ratti, just begun his Pontificate; and to Spain for a long and sunny honeymoon.

For long enough she used her accomplishments to entertain Loyola's guests, and indeed, it was only after nearly fifteen years of marriage and Ciarán and Deirdre were fourteen years of age that she began to get restive at Loyola's dinner parties and ceased to please his guests.

At a dinner to receive the Cultural Delegation of the Basque Republic to the People of Ireland, she insulted them, not the people of Ireland of whom she was bigotedly fond, but the Cultural Delegation.

This consisted of the Profesor of Middle Euskade Iambica, Bilbao University; a vice-president of the Basque Republic; his chaplain; the Secretary of the Catalan Committee for Joint Anti-Fascist Action of Trotskyites and Communists (3rd International); and Lady Jane Blanchard who spent a week trying to persuade W. B. Yeats to go out and fight in Easter Week 1916, and who was now on the Committee of the International Red Aid.

Lady Jane always insisted on giving this organisation its full name, in case it would be mistaken by its initials for the Irish Republican Army, with which she had fallen out in 1934, on the general question of the day-to-day struggle and the particular one of the I.R.A.'s refusal to spare a dozen twelve-ounce sticks of gelignite for a parcel to be sent to the Secretary of the Employers Federation during the coal strike.

The late Subhas Chandra Rose, the Indian Nationalist leader, described her, 'as a champion of the down-trodden in every land, a great friend of the Indian people, a fiery preacher for every good cause in her native land, the breaking-up of the big estates, the revival of the Irish language, and birth control – a splendid figure of revolting womanhood.'

Legend had it, that on occasion of her Easter visit, Yeats asked her what did she take him for, said he was too delicate a man and threw her down the stairs two days after the Fall of the General Post Office, because he was going to write a poem about it.

It was believed that she was instrumental in getting Frank Harris and Charlie Chaplin to visit Jim Larkin in Sing-Sing. She certainly used her influence with Governor Al Smith to get him out. Smith had an almost feudal regard for Lady Jane Blanchard, on account of her family having evicted his family from their cottage in County Cavan, back in the old days.

Apart from that (Loyola said), her great age would have entitled her to respect, apart from her life of service, when he described that terrible evening at the dinner party of the Cultural Delegation when María insulted them all.

At a party the previous week, for the All-Ireland Director of Operations for Standard Oil (New Jersey, U.S.A.) María showed signs of restlessness by leaving the dinner table before the tortilla. Loyola excused her by saying that she had a headache, and sweet things did not agree with her, and she was gone up to her room to lie down.

Now, many of the guests had on previous occasions seen her consume square yards of tortilla, of which she was extremely fond, and the fact that she had not gone up to her bedroom, but down to the kitchen, was made apparent to all assembled, by the rising notes of her fiddle on which she was playing the well-known tune, *Upstairs in a Tent*, for a hornpipe danced by the gardener's boy and a housemaid.

This was bad enough, though the party consisted of Dublin businessmen, who all suffered from their own wife troubles, but the next day, she announced to Loyola that she was sick and tired of his friends and acquaintances, and would he let her off those parties, and let her amuse herself with her own friends, in the kitchen.

'With the servants? ' asked Loyola.

'They are friends and relations, some of them of yours and mine,' said María.

'After all the money was spent on your rearing,' said he, 'your own second cousin in the Jockey Club de Buenos Aires – what are you? – beef to the heels, like a Mullingar heifer.'

He insisted, however, that she come to the next dinner party and they'd make arrangements about future dates. Most of the guests did not speak English, and she wouldn't have to be there to make conversation with the Cultural Delegation and the Secretary of the CCJAFATC (3rd Int.).

'All right,' said María, with resignation, 'if you say so, I'll make converstion with them.'

'You'll do as you're fuckingwell told,' said he, in Castilian.

María began by refusing to make conversation with either the Delegation or the Secretary of the CCJAFATC (3rd Int.) on the grounds that none of them spoke intelligible Spanish.

She offered a handkerchief to the Chairman of the Cultural Delegation, because she said she did not wish him to blow his nose on his napkin.

As Loyola said, she spared neither age nor the sanctity of God's anointed for she called Lady Jane an old Grange bitch, and alleged that the chaplain, sitting beside her, was trying to feel her leg under the table.

'You might at least have respect for Father Cardona's Sacred Office,' said Loyola, with mounting fury.

'He might keep his Sacred Paws to himself,' said María, 'Catholics . . . Catholics how are you! This crowd is no better than the Christian Front.'

This was a reference to the crowd supporting Franco, ex-members of the British police force, the Royal Irish Constabulary, and their sons, with some ex-Free State Army officers, and failed clerical students, though the mass of them were recruited from the Dublin underworld.

They were known to the Franco Army as 'the tourists' and their leader, General O'Duffy, as 'the Flying Postman,' because he went around in an aeroplane collecting his men's mail, while his men spent their time reading and writing letters and sending postcards home, drinking cheap wine and smoking cigarettes.

Six hundred of them left Ireland, and all returned safely but seven, six of whom were killed accidentally. The other one was in a bad state of health for some years before he joined the force, and only went to Spain because his parish priest thought the climate might do him good.

It was a deadly insult, to compare a bourgeois Nationalist, or any respectable person, (even a respectable supporter of Franco), whose family had not been in the Black and Tans or convicted of burglary or shop-lifting or living on prostitutes with the Christian Front.

By the grace of Providence the guests did not know this, nor notice the insults at all, nor the altercation between Mr. and Mrs. Bolívar. The Iberians could not understand English and gave determined attention to the food and wine. Lady Jane was stone deaf and very drunk. So that dinner party did not pass off so very disastrously, but at the next, María dropped the Ibizenco fish-weight on the head of the President of the Scottish Widows' Mutual Financial Trust; he was unconscious for four days, and Mr. and Mrs. Bolívar finally parted.

Loyola was a generous man to his family and María was not short of money herself. She moved out of the big house, in County Dublin, and bought one for herself in Ballsbridge. Here she lived, with Ciarán and Deirdre, and her uncle Hymie. Ciarán and Deirdre were away at school when their father and mother parted, but it was agreed that María should have the custody of them.

Loyola was kind and sent them money, but he was the kind of man that needed his children about him, although he was satisfied that they were being well looked after.

When they finished boarding-school and went to the National University, Loyola called at the house in Ballsbridge one day, held a conference with María, and presented them with a new motor-cycle to take them to and from their classes. Ciarán was to drive it, and Deirdre was to go pillion. Sometime Ciarán had another girl called Mairéad Callan as a pillion passenger, but Deirdre did not object, because she had affairs of her own to attend to.

Ciarán was studying medicine, and Deirdre was studying Social Science, because she wanted to work with little children. Her brother remarked, grimly, that she would not be short of a supply of them, by the looks of things. This was what the party was about.

In the years they were growing up, their father continued to take an active interest in them and in plans for their futures. He had fixed it already for Ciarán to take over a doctor's practice as soon as he had qualified. He did not think much of Deirdre's Social Science, and when she was eighteen she was introduced to a very correct, well-dressed young man from the Mexican Embassy, whose family was rotten with money.

There was no difficulty in the way, for María agreed with Loyola that it was an excellent match. Deirdre, dear, amiable and healthy girl, smiled when he asked her to marry him, and said she'd love to.

He was very formal, but most attentive. He called and took her out in his car every Sunday. The wedding was fixed for Saint Stephen's Day, the twenty-sixth of December, a favourite day for Irish weddings, and an engagement of one year.

But between hopping and trotting, Deirdre had been seeing this student from National, and his foot slipped.

By this month of September she was discovered to

be somewhat pregnant.
This was where I came in.

I had been a comrade of Ciarán's in the Fianna Boys – the Irish Republican youth organisation – since we were twelve years old, and later in the I.R.A. We were both twenty-one; he was a third year medical student, and I was following the family trade of house-painting. Ciarán and I drank together, and sometimes I drank with Deirdre – not that she drank much.

I did not drink with her and Ciarán together, except in their house, for he was a bit of a snob and did not want his only sister to get involved with a house-painter, if she could get some fellow with the readies.

I visited the house and went to all their parties. Deirdre liked me a lot, Mairéad said I did Deirdre a lot of good, and was worth listening to, except when I was drunk, and Ciarán liked me a lot, because we were old comrades and as long as I did not attempt to involve myself with his sister.

I liked them all but I am a proud man, and the last I resented.

They all certainly liked me, except the old one's and Loyola's love for their children and, it may be mentioned, friendship for each other was only equalled by their disapproval of me as a friend for them.

María's disapproval changed to dislike when I went to her house in my professional capacity to wallpaper a room.

She came down and asked me what I would like for my dinner, it being Friday. She was ever-generous with food and drink. She was never sure, she said, what religion I was. The old cow, and all belonging to me Catholics since 432 A.D. But I knew fish was scarce and not good that week, so I said I was a Protestant, and she gave me a steak.

Later she discovered that I was not a Protestant, whatever I was, but a Catholic, and she denounced me to the children, and said I had sold Jesus Christ for threequarters of a pound of beef, and must never darken her door again. I don't think she ever liked me darkening it, at that. But when this matter of Deirdre's came up, Ciarán came looking for me to do something about it, and I did.

María, through some way of her own, known only to religious people, pretended to think that Deirdre was only going on a holiday, though none of that household had ever used England for holidays, other than as a stepping-stone to Paris, Rome or Barcelona. She financed the trip to Bristol, and even said to Deirdre at the Airport, 'Now, enjoy yourself, *a stór.* *'

I was welcomed back to the house shortly after that, and once more was a welcome guest there any time I was too drunk to make my way home from a party.

And this, the evening of Deirdre's return, I was welcomed with open arms by her brother, who threw them round me, and María gave me qualified approval and a glass of whiskey.

In a corner and blind-drunk as he had been for sixty years, was uncle Hymie.

He was the second most blasphemous man I'd ever met, except during his hangover in the morning.

71

Before he'd got a few glasses of whiskey into him he'd moan and groan about his past and sinful life, and quite sincerely pour himself a couple to give him the strength to get down to Mass. But by the time he had recovered sufficiently to get as far as the church door, he was strong in his unbelief again, and very coarse apart from blasphemous.

When I walked in, he said to me, 'How is the hammer hanging?' adding in the same breath, 'Deirdre is on the telephone talking to her intended. She looks well after her trip to the other side.'

'Why wouldn't she look well?' said I, 'and she a fine girl not twenty years of age? Aren't you looking well, and you four times that age?'

'I am by Jasus,' said Uncle Hymie, 'and six more years with it.'

I knew he was eighty-five years old or more. He left the County Kildare the time of the Land War, in Parnell's day. Hymie shot a landlord who was evicting a widow and six small children, and had to leave the country like many a decent man before and since.

He went to Dublin on the run there, till the money would arrive from Mexico to take him to his people there.

In the meantime, there was this fine summer's day, and he went taking the fresh air for himself up in the Phoenix Park, and stood for a while watching a cricket match. One of the gentlemen players hit the ball, and it travelled about two hundred yards and looked like travelling another two hundred. Hymie walked casually along the side of the field almost as soon as the ball left the bat and reached up and caught it.

The gentry were in amazement and came over to

72

ask him whether he would care to join in a game, when one of their number stepped up beside him, slipped him a gold sovereign and said, in a low tone, 'Get out of here, you bloody ruffian, while you're safe. The Vice-Regal Lodge is only a few yards from here.'

'How do you know me?' asked Uncle Hymie.

'Bloody well, I know you,' says the gentleman. 'Isn't it many's the time I saw you playing on the estate team. Only Hymie Bolívar could field a ball like that.'

Hymie nodded to him, and went off out of the Park as quickly as he could with his sovereign.

I never heard Hymie tell the story himself, though I heard him tell plenty of lies, but I knew that story was true because I heard it from other people.

When the Irish Free State was established in 1922, Hymie came home from Mexico. He applied for a pension for his part in the Land War, and discovered that the official he gave an account of his deed to was a nephew of the landlord he'd shot.

He lived for some time with his sister, back in the County Kildare, but had to leave her place and come to María's place in Dublin, on account of a terrible thing he did on the poor woman and she lying ill in bed. The sister used to get people to read to her; books of devotion mostly, and prayers of a consolatory nature, to prepare her for the next world and ease her passage from this.

Hymie went to the library and out of a pile of old books picked an antique volume with a leather cover. He told the sister it was *The Imitation of Christ* by Thomas à Kempis. He told her that when they opened his coffin to see whether his remains were incorrupt it was discovered that he had been buried alive, by the fact that he had gnawed away the top of his right shoulder, presumably in a frenzy when he woke up and found himself to have been buried.

Hymie told the terrified sister that the same thing happened Juarez, the great Jesuit theologian.

Then he read her a piece from his venerable leather-covered book: "It is well remembered here that, about seven years ago, one Frolick, a tall boy with lank hair, remarkable for stealing eggs and fucking them, was taken from the school in this parish..."

'Be Christ, and that's a remarkable thing,' he says to the pour ould one in the bed, '"eggs, eggs". I've heard of many things in my day between here and Casa Catalina's but "eggs", that's a new one on me. I wonder how he managed it?'

I was thinking that myself, when he asked me. 'I hear you do a bit of writing?'

'A bit,' said I.

"I seen a thing in one of them magazines they prints on straw or something, in this miserable country, about you being in prison in England for the cause.'

'Like John Devoy, the Fenian – *Recollections of an Irish Rebel*, and all goddam lies. Every whoring thing in it.

'I met him in 'Frisco in 'eighty-nine, when he came down from New York, with a lot of other gringo tinkers looking for subscriptions for Parnell. Myself and another young fellow, Argentine-Irish, were after coming from Mexico City to meet them, to hand over a big collection of money from Irish in America del Scot...'

'From where?'

'America, Latin America, the respectable bit. Anyway this boy with me was of a very old family, and could speak nothing but Spanish. There was a Bowery Boy with Devoy, and when he heard Patricio speak to me in Spanish he says, 'Who is the greaser? I thought this was a *Clann na nGael** meeting.'

"This boy's name is O'Brien," said I, "I don't know what yours is, you Yankee scum."

"Now, now," says Devoy, "no fighting for God's sake," and turning to the other fellow, "I'll explain in a minute. But they'll only say here, it's the Irish again, fighting amongst themselves."

'He was a cute little bastard all right, and settled the row and collected the *dinero* off of us.'

'But,' said Hymie, with a hard look at me, 'you're writing your *Recollections of an Irish Rebel* before you've had any goddam recollections – at twenty years of age!'

'I'm twenty-one,' said I.

'Well, twenty-one. The way Ciarán talks about you, anyone would think you were Robert Emmet on a white mare. How the hell did you do three years in English jails, if you are only twenty-one?"

'I was sixteen when I was sentenced.'

'In this paper you were writing it says ...'

'Listen Hymie, never mind my writing. How about your reading? What was the book you read to your sister with the dirt in it?'

'There was no dirt whatsoever in it, though you are all so pig ignorant. It was *The Rambler* by Doctor Samuel Johnson, A Londoner's Visit to the Country, if you want to know.

So it was too, when I looked it up a few nights

after, in the National Library.

'Have another drink, Brendan Behan,' said María. She always called me by my two names, so as to be polite, but at the same time not making too free with me.

'I will, ma'am, thank you,' said I, 'I'd sooner the Vartry water than the soda water, if it's all equal to you.'

'For me, María, um, ah, whiskey solo,' said Hymie, holding out his tumbler.

'You've had your 'nough for the moment,' said María.

'Ah, María, your poor ould Tee Ah Och Aye me.' (That's how it sounded).

She handed me a drink.

'May the giving hand never falter,' said I.

You're welcome this night, Brendan Behan. Take what you like out of that. Any other night, I supposed, the water out of the tap would be good enough for me. But like that again, that was not true either. Fair play is bonny play, and one thing about María or anyone belonging to her, they were never mean with drink.

Hymie put forward his glass again and she refilled it, and her own, with resignation.

'Salud and sláinte,' said María.

'Sláinte 'gus saol agaibh,'* said I.

'Salud, sláinte, muchas pesetas,' said Hymie adding something about my castinettas.

'That'll do you now,' said María, 'mind yourself. An old man like you, should be ashamed of yourself. On your knees you should be thinking of the next

76

world.'

'I thought that was supposed to be a great place,' said Hymie.

'It depends which part of it you go to,' said María.

'Be Jasus, and the Pope mustn't think much of his chances of going to the good part, for there's no great hurry on him going there. Any time he's sick there's about fifty medicos from every part of the world in attendance on him, whether it's his arse or his elbow.'

'Now, Uncle,' said María, severely.

'What was that he said in Spanish about castin-ettas?' I asked her.

'Don't have me tell you,' said she, 'it was shocking anyway.'

'Well,' said Hymie, 'what would shock that fellow would turn thousands grey. I only said . . .'

'Never you mind what you only said,' said María. 'Tomorrow morning when you wake up, craw-sick, you'll be down on your knees, praying for the wrath of God to be averted from a sinful old man. I know,' she added, 'because I've heard you in your room.'

'Seeing as you listen to my prayers, it's a wonder you wouldn't be listening outside the retrate* as well, when I'd be relieving myself of a morning.'

Hymie's humour had changed. He was really annoyed.

'Look,' said I, 'here's the girl herself.' Deirdre was coming down the stairs. 'Fresh and well she's looking after her trip.'

'So well she might,' muttered Hymie. María left us, to bring Deirdre over to someone to introduce them.

'Hymie,' said I, 'Deirdre is very fond of you.'

'Nobody's fond of you when you are old,' said he, 'the only reason the other bitch has me here is because she can call me Uncle, and it makes her think she's still young.'

When her introductions to the new guest were complete, Deirdre came over to us. Her black hair gleaming, brushed back the way she always wore it, her oval face and brown eyes shining, innocent and understanding. The Madonna.

I was not thinking of her recent adventure, and certainly I was not thinking in sarcasm.

If she couldn't resist a fellow, it was because she was too kind.

'Feel better, now dear,' is a cant phrase, but in Deirdre's case, it was an exact description of her maternal attitude. Not exactly, because she had her own enjoyment too, and I know she had that as part of and as much as the head stroking and consoling.

As natural and as pure as spring water, and I'd have done a lot for her, and did. Wasn't I after organising what even to me, a bad Catholic, was a most grievous sin?

'Well, *a mhic*,' she looked at me, 'How's Brendan?'

'Couldn't be better,' said I, 'if I was any better, I couldn't stick it. You're looking smashing, Deirdre, after your trip.'

She gave a class of a look more humourous than a wink, and said, 'Why wouldn't I?'

'You took the words out of me mouth,' said Hymie, who still had the spite, over María's remarks to him.

'You could offer Deirdre a more civil welcome than that,' said I.

'Oh,' said Deirdre, 'my Uncle Hymie welcomed me already. He was out at the airport with Ciarán and Mammy fighting,' she turned to Hymie, who grunted.

78

'I'll get a drink for the three of us. Malt, Brendan; and you, Uncle? We have to ask the guests before the family. Malt? Right. And I'll have a Cork Gin and tonic, and it looks like water, crystal clear, so as the people won't know what I'm drinking.'

We watched her at the sideboard. She poured a good measure of gin for herself.

'For a girl of nineteen,' said I, 'she's not a bad hand at filling them.'

'She's not, then, God bless her,' said Uncle Hymie.

'She never was though,' said I, 'she takes it as she takes everything, as something that is there to be enjoyed. I saw her when she was seventeen drink as much as any of us, cook us a breakfast of rashers and eggs and then ask us all to go swimming, and we lying half-dead trying to swallow a curer.'

'It's the likes of you has her the way she is,' said Hymie, 'her and Ciarán,' he added, begrudgingly.

'Oh, I shouldn't have said that,' said I, 'about her drinking as much as any of us; I forgot that you're her grand-uncle,'

I forgot, said I, in my own mind, that you are a dying old bollocks, and that I'm only pleasing you, by drawing attention to your relationship to this lovely girl – lovely, in the way that bright eyes and softness and breasts and humour and good opening legs made her. You, said I to Hymie, are as much a relation of hers as what the man in the moon, whoever in Jasus's name he is, is. Fucked up and dried up long since you are.

She came back anyway with the drinks, and Hymie forgot his bad humour, talking and drinking again. And I forgot mine. Couldn't I afford to? Poor old wretch. We all live to be as old as we can.

Lifting my tumbler I said to Deirdre, *'Céad míle fáilte* – a hundred thousand welcomes to you, and you home.'

*'Go raibh míle maith agat, a Bhreandáin,'** said she, 'it's great to be home. Oh, there's Mairéad.' She took a running dive from Hymie and me, and went over to Mairéad Callan who was coming in the hall.

There was a confusion of female embracing and clinching and, 'Oh, Deirdre, you look marvellous,' and more clinching and kissing, and 'Oh, Mairéad, it's lovely to see you,' and 'Oh, Deirdre, the trip did you good,' and 'Let me touch you.'

'My Deirdre, and how you've grown,' I muttered, watching this touching scene.

'What's that you said? ' said Hymie.

'How about a rozziner? ' said I.

'Musha then, it wouldn't kill us,' said Hymie.

I brought over a whiskey bottle and filled our two tumblers.

'Hombre,' said Hymie.

'The skin off your knackers,' said I.

Deirdre and Mairéad broke from their clinch.

'Well, Brendan,' said Mairéad, with heaving bosom, 'and how are you?'

'Only look at me,' said I.

'Good evening, Mr. Bolívar,' said she, paying her respects to Hymie.

'Ciarán is doing barman,' said Deirdre, 'he'll be over in a minute.'

'It's not him I came to see at all,' said Mairéad, with tempered judgement, 'but yourself, Deirdre.'

'Oh, is that the way with you,' said I, 'are you long going together?'

'I can see Ciarán any time,' said Mairéad.

Ciarán joined us then and from that out the five of us were together.

María was well on, and after a while got out the fiddle and a fellow from their part of the country came out with an accordion and we danced and had a great *céilí**.

Most of the guests were students at the National University and friends of the Bolívars from the rich plains of the Midlands and had every look of solid comfort about them.

They had two ways of looking at me. They liked me, because I had served a sentence of three years for possessing explosives, but they didn't like the fact that I was a Dublin jackeen*. They applauded vociferously when I sang nationalist songs about the 1916 Rising, but when I sang songs about the 1913 General Strike, they were only polite.

Hymie had it both ways, and every way. He sang songs about the Land War, and with these students the memory of shooting English landlords was a worthy thing to be well remembered, but to go on strike against an Irish capitalist was not the same thing..

I did not blame them for that. Many of them were the sons of gombeen-men, credit shopkeepers and moneylenders getting the profits of a whole district each containing maybe a thousand families, and some of their ancestors, at any rate, had suffered a lot under the landlords.

Hymie sang: 'Oh, and sure if he spent it on mountainy dew
I'd sooner he drank nor gave it to you.
You're a rent agent get* should be hung from a yew

81

tree, says the wife of the Bould Tenant Farmer.'
and the lament for Lord Waterford, a big landowner:
'"Oh, Lord Watherford is dead", says the Shan
Van Vocht
"Oh, Lord Watherford is dead", says the Shan Van
Vocht.
"Lord Watherford is dead and the devil make his
bed,
With an oven for his head", says the Shan Van
Vocht.'
'Go on, Hymie, you boy, you,' they shouted.
'"The first that he did see," says the Shan Van
Vocht,
"Was his bailiff Black Magee," says the Shan Van
Vocht.
"He was standing at the shelf, washing up the divil's
delf,"
Says he, "Milord, is that yourself?" says the Shan
Van Vocht,
"Milord, is that yourself?" says the Shan Van
Vocht.'
'Me life on you, Hymie!' they shouted, 'your
blood is worth bottling!' Well, just at the moment it
might be, for his old face was pink as a baby's from
passion and drink.
'Glory-o! Glory-o! to her brave sons who died,
in the cause of long down-trodden Man.
Glory-o! to Mount Leinster's own darling and pride
Dauntless Kelly, the boy from Killann.'
So we all got well oiled, and Ciarán, as I knew he
would, began remembering when we were kids in the
Fianna, and Frank Ryan and Eamonn McGrotty, our
leaders, went out with the International Brigade,
leaving us who were fourteen years of age with the

women and children, and a humiliating place for tough chisellers* like us. We were left collecting tinned milk and packets of cocoa and bags of flour for the Foodship and were only consoled by street fights, stone-throwing, and one fatal (for them) shooting encounter with the Duffy gang.

So, Ciarán starts crying about all the poor kids, some of them only a couple of years older than ourselves that were killed at University City, Albacete, Brunette, Guadalajara, and Ciarán is there crying like the rain over them.

But I know that it's not the dead Fianna boys he is thinking of mostly, but it's his father he is crying for, blood being thicker than politics.

'Go on, Brendan,' he roars, 'give us another one.'

So, encouraged like that again, I start off with songs from the Spanish War-time, about Duffy, and his crusaders for France, and some of the fellows at the party did not like them, on account of being of the big farming class that the Blue Shirts* came out of, but they had to put up with it.

'Sure, with money lent by Vickers,
We can buy blue shirts and knickers,
Let the Barcelona Bolshies, take a warning,
Though his feet are full of bunions,
Still he knows his Spanish onions,
And we're off to Salamanca in the morning.'

The bit about his feet was a reference to the fact that O'Duffy was Chief of the Free State police for ten years.

'No Pasarán!' shouted Ciarán, but his friends and relations were not overpleased. They clapped politely, though one of them, in an accent like a bullock said, 'You could let the dead rest all the same.'

'Arra, fuck him,' said I, coarsely.

'Go on, Brendan,' shouted Ciarán, urging me on to further excesses, and leading the song himself this time:

'Adelante pueblo, Bandera Roja
Bandera Roja, triunfará ...
Viva la República y la Libertad!'

'No Pasarán!' shouted María absently, and then recollecting her domestic grievance, 'Ah, can't you give us an Irish song, Brendan Behan.'

So we all got friendly and soft *súgach** drunk, and everyone friendly with everyone else, which is the happiest thing we have in this world, although not always easy or certain to come by, till we sang the last coherent melody, we who had not passed out beyond all hope of recognition:

'Come, come beautiful Eileen, come for a drive with me,
Over the mountains, down by the fountains,
Up by the highways, and down by the byways,
Make up your mind, don't be unkind
And we'll drive to Castlebar.
On the road there's no danger, to me you're no stranger,
So, up like a bird on me ould jaunting car.'

Then most of the guests departed, and there was the noise of cars starting and shouts of who wants a lift here, and you move over there and take Noreen on your knees and no carrying on under the rugs please, keep your hands easy, I can't get her started and you're awful, get out and push, and then silence, and there was only a few of us left.

I found myself, as often I found myself before, in an armchair with Deirdre on my lap and her arms tangled round me, and in an adjoining armchair like the other half of a family group were Ciarán and Mairéad in a similar position. Mairéad was lighter than Deirdre. This I did not know from experience, because Mairéad was strict and impatient. Though frail and fair, she could repulse a pass from another fellow as effectively as she could a warning or advice about her affair with Ciarán.

She laughed at me as if I were twelve years old, except when I was talking about books or plays for she took me very seriously as a writer, but as a man, not at all.

I was not satisfied with this because, like everyone in this world, I wanted respect for other things besides those qualities I was sure of.

I suppose on balance I preferred Deirdre because I was not afraid of her.

But this I must say, that no two people even if one was as light as Mairéad, ever slept in eachother's arms. There's no sleeping about it, except in an armchair or the back of a car, and then only for the woman, for the man is a mattress for her. Lying here this night, I was cramped as the crucified, and then only able to move my arm, and yawn restrictedly.

I heard a steady snoring from the other side of the room, and some anguished muttering.

María was doing the snoring, and Uncle Hymie the anguishing; 'Oh, Lord Jesus, into Thy Hands I commend my spirit. Lord Jesus take me to Yourself.'

'Amen to that, you noisy old fucker, as quick as He likes, but do you want to wake up the other old bitch on us?'

María was stirring, like a dog digesting a dinner. Deirdre woke and whispered, 'It's very late, pet, you'll stay the night?' I nodded. My oath.

'Mammy says you can stay with Ciarán. Mairéad is staying with me in my room,' and she moved off and went to wake the others.

The others shook themselves up and we crept along to our rooms.

'Goodnight, Brendan; goodnight, Ciarán; Mairéad and I are going to my room now.'

In our room I looked round and sat on the bed beside the wall next to the girls' room.

'No,' said Ciarán, 'the other bed is yours.'

I went to the other bed and sat down.

'We'd better get into bed quick,' said Ciarán. 'That light is annoying me.'

'I was waiting on the girls to use the Jacks* first,' said I.

'Never mind that. They can go upstairs if they want, though they're probably waiting on us to use it. We'll go down now.'

We went down and came back. I threw off my clothes, and got into bed.

'Why the hell don't you hang your clothes up?' said Ciarán. 'There are clothes-hooks there in the corner.'

'I did hang them up,' said I, 'on the floor where they can't fall off.'

'Why the hell can't you act like anybody else. You've brains to burn, God knows, but shaving about once a fortnight, and acting like these bloody Baggot Street Bohemians . . .'

'Drums is our team,' said I, 'not Bohemians.' Drumcondra and Bohemians were also the name of Soccer teams. 'Bohs are amateurs, gentlemen players from the University not long off the bog, and doing

86

their medical course with the money their daddies robbed off of the starving peasantry.'

'Oh, for Jesus's sake,' said Ciarán, 'doing the downtrodden proletariat again? Are my pyjamas under your pillow?'

They were. 'I didn't think you'd need them,' said I. He looked at me. 'What do you mean by that?'

'It's a hot night,' I said, *'oíche mhaith dhuit.***'

Ciarán put out the light. *'Oíche mhaith dhuit.'*

I lay in the dark looking up at the top of the window, and heard Ciarán breathe deeply to himself. God give you patience.

'Hey, Brendan,' he said in a hoarse whisper – that's what he said it in, 'Do you think my ma is gone to bed yet?'

'Whether she's in bed or on the sofa, she's put out the light,' said I.

'O.K. Would you mind going out for a bit?'

'Not at all. I'll put on my pants and socks and scarper.'

'And what?'

'Scarper – my old reform school slang, "scarper". Some says it's short for the rhyming slang for "Scapa Flow," meaning "go." Others say it's Italian for "go."''

'Never mind that, now, just do it.'

'I'm dressed, ready and all.'

I got out of bed and went into the hall. I stood there for a minute, and then decided to pass the time by going to the Jacks. Besides it was useful and necessary. Our organs can stand many and various things, but they are cinema organs, which is not much of a joke, but the best I could do at that hour, and my cerebralities taxed to the full with blood rushing from my stomach.

When I came out, I stood outside Deirdre's door, and Mairéad at last sneaked out.

She was wearing a sort of tennis nightie which consists of, to the best of my knowledge and belief, a frock of white cotton with no arms, with rows of shamrocks all over it, and a collar with double the ration of shamrocks to the square inch and some crosses.

'The changing of the guard,' said I.

'Hurry up and get in out of the cold,' said she, not haughtily but reasonably, like one talking to an unreasonable, though not unlikable, person.

'I will so,' said I, and went into Deirdre's room. For the sake of good manners, and curiosity, I went over first to the other bed beside our wall.

It had not been slept in. I made my way over to Deirdre's bed and slipped in beside her.

A tragedy of this life, I found out, is that you never realise how young you are, till you are not so young, and then (I suppose) when you are old.

We were barely lying along thighs, starboard to port, so to speak, when María struggled up and came gasping and snorting and panting along the corridor, and shouted, 'Brendan Behan, where are you?'

'I'm here, in bed, in Ciarán's room.'

'Mairéad?' bellowed the old bellowdame.

'Yes, María. I'm here with Deirdre,' she shouted from beside her naked (I presume) fiancé.

The old one shambled away to her drunken sleep. 'That's right, I'll allow no hedging or ditching in this house, to bring the curse of God on us. It's not lucky, but you are all good children. Boys with boys, and girls with girls, what's natural and decent. That's the motto and sleeping arrangements of this house, and of every decent Catholic home.' She went off muttering to herself. 'Nice Irish dances, no lying on top of, and eating, one another. As poor Father Ignatius Mary used to say, 'Fun, yes, but fun without vulgarity...'

'That's it,' I murmured.

'What's that, pet?' asked Deirdre.

'I'll tell you in a second,' said I, adding, of course, a term of endearment.

The rest of the night I describe with these dots ...... and, of course, some sleep.

In the morning, Deirdre got up to cook the breakfasts. Mairéad came in, and said, 'Get up and go into your own room. I want to get into bed before María comes down.'

I stretched my arms from the bed, 'Come in, and welcome.'

'Come on, Funny Wonder,' said Mairéad, impatiently, 'it's cold out here.'

I got upstairs, and into Ciarán's room, and into my own bed. He turned and groaned, 'Dear Lord, I could do with a drink.'

'That's a funny thing. I bet you didn't think about it at all till Mairéad got up; after that the horn is part of the hangover, like the itch.'

'A lot of good Deirdre going away, and the first thing she does is to sleep the night with you.'

'What did you want me to do? Stand out in the corridor all night?'

'There were two beds there. You could have slept in Mairéad's.'

'And how do you know I didn't?'

'Bloodywell, I know you didn't. You'd get up on a cat.'

'Such is not my reputation around Baggot Street. There the intelligensia-esses think I am slow, if not positively King Lear.'

'Well,' he admitted, 'looking at those ones with their Egyptian jewellery and woollen stockings, I wouldn't blame you. But it could be very awkward about Deirdre and you.'

'What about yourself and Mairéad kipped in there for the night?'

'That's a different thing. We're engaged to be married, and a month or two wouldn't make any difference one way or another.'

'Well, I wouldn't object to marrying Deirdre.'

'No, but my mother would, and to be straight with you so would I.'

'Much about you,' said I, 'or your old one either.'

'Well, what the hell could you do for her? I know and she knows and my mother knows that you've a great talent as a writer, but you can't treat that. It might be years before you made a living at it, if you ever did. And in the meantime you won't work at your trade of house-painting. But to hell with that. I always liked you since we were kids in the Fianna together, and I like you now, even though you get fighting drunk and use bad language before women. At the back of it, we're bourgeois people. And you? Well according to yourself, you're a jackeen from the North City Slums. It's only your own description I'm using.'

'You're not bourgeois,' said I, 'Yours are worse, yours are bloody bogmen, or bogmen and bog-women, and the cowshit barely off of your boots, talking to the likes of me whose people, seed, breed and generation, are in this town since yours came out of your mud cabins – you consumptive poxy parcel of fuckpigs.'

I was dressed by this time, and went out, slamming the door behind me.

'Hey, Brendan,' Ciarán shouted after me, 'wait a minute.'

But I went downstairs to the kitchen to say goodbye to Deirdre.

She was in the kitchen talking over the stove with Mairéad who was laying the table.

'Good morning all,' said I.

'You too,' said Mairéad.

'Ah there you are, Brendan,' said Deirdre, in her easy gentle way. 'You're just in time for your breakfast.'

'I don't want any, thanks.'

'You don't want any? Sure it's ready, and the tea is wet, and all.'

'I'm in a hurry out,' said I, in a sulky tone, so as they would know there was something up.

'It's not out to work you're going? ' said Mairéad.

'You mind your own fuckin' business,' said I. 'That's what you'll do.'

'Don't talk to me like that,' said this stern, slim, fair-haired girl, 'or I'll throw a plate at you.'

'What's wrong with you, pet? ' asked Deirdre, to coax me. 'Sure no one's been saying anything to you?'

'It's just that I'm going off now, goodbye.'

I went out of the kitchen, but slowly up the stairs. I heard Mairéad say, unconcernedly, 'It suits him to go off like that.'

But Deirdre replied in a scornful, grieved, and troubled tone, something that I could not hear. But it was the tone that I cared about, and I walked with a surer step.

María met me at the top of the stairs, and I must say that for an elderly woman that was after a bellyful of booze the previous night, she looked very well.

'Did you sit and have your breakfast, Brendan Behan?' she asked.

'No, thanks ma'am, I'm in a bit of a hurry.' So, I was, for the smell of food was making me sick, and I could not eat anything till I'd got a few drinks into me. That was really why I did not stay for breakfast, though I was hoping to get a bit of consideration for my wounded pride at the same time.

'Well, anyway, my husband sent you a message,' said she.

'A message from García?"

'His name is not García, but Loyola. Though he had a first cousin in Córdoba – not Córdoba in Spain, but Córdoba in Mexico – that was called García, García Francisco de Torres Maloney – a lovely step dancer he was too. He could dance *The Top of the Cork Road* better than any other boy in the whole of Mexico. Though I didn't know you ever heard of him, you must have heard Ciarán talking about him.'

'That was it,' said I.

'Well anyway, my husband sent you this message.'

She handed me an envelope.

'Thank you, ma'am, I'll see if there's an answer to it.'

I went into the Catalonian Cabinet Room, and opened it. Inside was a blue ten pound note. I put it in my pocket. There was no other message. I got a piece of notepaper, put that in the envelope and went back to María. 'Here,' said I, giving her back the envelope, 'tell Mr. Bolívar thanks very much, but I'm not in his employment. He can keep his money.'

'But – but – listen,' said María, 'he only wants to . . .'

'Thanks,' said I, my inexorable hand upraised, 'and good morning. I'm in a hurry.'

So I was, and for three reasons. I was afraid she would look into the envelope and find that I'd taken the ten pound note; I was afraid if I delayed any longer I'd get sick in front of her; and I was in a hurry to get down the Markets for a drink.

'Arra, *Dia dhuit*,' says Mick to me. A nice old skin, though I'd sooner heathens than publicans. 'God bless you.'

'*Dia 's Muire dhuit, 's Padraig, 's Bríd, 's Colmchille dhuit-se, a Mhíchil, agus do chuile dhuine macánta san teach seo.*'

'God and Mary and Patrick, Bridget, and Colmcille to yourself, Michael, and to every decent person in this house.'

The crowd lined up at the bar, and sitting in a row along the wall, intoned the responses. 'Amen, amen,' answered the porter sharks, whiskey kings, wine lords and cider barons. And Michael the publican added, 'Amen, *a Thiarna Dhia*,' 'Amen, O Lord God,' for he was a genuine religious man, and one of the few religious men that was not a worse bastard than ordinary people.

Doctor Crippen made room for me at the bar, and MacIntaggart the other side of me. Beside them I stood, like Christ between the two thieves.

Doctor Crippen's real name I did not know. He got his nickname from the time he was a barman in a

Free State Army canteen and was said to have poisoned the soldiers with bad drink. It was said that he killed more that way than the I.R.A. whom they were fighting at the time.

MacIntaggart's name in Irish is *Mac an tSagairt,* or 'son of the priest.' Some tease from Connemara told him this; since then he'd gone round the gullible public that he was the son of a bloody priest. Not that anyone in the Markets would believe the Lord's Prayer from his mouth. If you asked MacIntaggart the time, you'd check it on the telephone, if you wanted the right time.

Crippen, in his day, was a sergeant-major in the Free State Army and played Gaelic football for the Army Metro, who were drawn from the barracks of the Dublin Metropolitan Garrison. Michael, the publican, respected him greatly for his former glory on the football field, but Crippen did not know this. He was a humble and simple soul, and only told lies in the way of business, to get a drink, a feed or the price of his keep.

The only thing I knew him to boast about was his association with a literary magazine called *The Bat* and his friendship with the associate editor, Ernest Simms.

The editor was a little left wing Republican from an island in the Atlantic ocean off the coast of West Cork. He began writing when he came out of jail in the twenties and Ireland had still a vogue amongst the English writing and reading class, on account of the Black and Tans putting Ireland on the Liberal Conscience.

Like all the other peasant writers, he was an ex-schoolmaster, and wrote lovingly about simple folk of his native place. I could make neither head nor tail of what any of them wrote and this editor suspected as much. He did not like me for it, nor my bits of short stories would he publish.

A coffee drinker and a hater of liquor, he liked Crippen not at all.

But the associate editor, a big hardy boy that boxed for Trinity College, was one of the gentlest people that I have ever met. He was a Protestant clergyman's son, and had a mania for backing horses. This was shared by Crippen, who adored him, and every time we met Crippen recalled the memory of his friend.

To finance their respective speculations, Simms removed the postage stamps from the stamped addressed envelopes enclosed for the return of their contributions, if rejected, by intending authors. They also removed International Reply Coupons from mss., for these were also acceptable in the bookies that Crippen ran too.

In this way they had made a half a crown on the nose for the jolly favourite at Epsom or Aintree.

Crippen had a conscientious objection to backing on Irish racing which, he said, was run dishonestly.

'Well,' said Crippen, as I knew he would, 'give us a drink, how is Ernie Simms?' In the one breath like that.

'Give the Doctor a pint of stout, Michael, and I'll have a half of malt for myself. What are you having?' I asked MacIntaggart.

'Hard times,' said he.

'Give him a pint of stout,' said I.

'How is Ernie Simms?' asked Crippen again.

'He's all right,' said I, 'he's over in London working for the B.B.C. He's on the Third Programme.'

'Hmm,' said Crippen, sagaciously, 'and the same fellow could be on the First, if only he minded himself.'

The phone rang, and Stinking Fish called me.

He was an old gurrier* that got his name from the time it was only legal for people who do business in the markets to drink there in the early morning. Stinking used to have a basket of old fish that had been discarded as unfit for human consumption, and he'd sell it to the people. When a policeman came round and asked them what they were doing in the market, they'd hold up their piece of stinking fish and say, 'I'm a buyer.'

'I'll see if Mr. Brendan Behan is here,' said Stinking Fish, looking over at me, and shouted alongside the receiver, 'Is Mr. Behan there?' I nodded and Stinking said, 'I think Mr. Behan is here. Yes, he is, and will take a message. Here he is now.' He handed me the phone, 'Here you are, Mr. Behan, sir.'

It was Ciarán.

'Listen, what the hell do you mean by telling my mother that you wouldn't take money from my father?'

'Why should I take money from any of you pack of fucking cowboys?'

'But you *did* take it after insulting the woman.'

'You're a fucking liar. I opened the envelope and handed it back to her after I saw what was in it.'

'After you took the ten pounds out of it.'

'I did not. I handed the envelope back to her, as I got it.'

'With the ten pounds gone and a piece of notepaper you put in its place.'

'That's what she told you. You're a liar, and she's a

liar and a thief.'

'And you're a rotten fucking bastard, and I was worse ever to have anything to do with you. Fuck you!'

'You, too, and your friends in America, and your blind aunt in Spiddal!'

He banged down the receiver in a fury, and I went back to the bar.

'The same again, Michael,' said I, 'and a drink for Stinking Fish.'

'Thanks,' said Stinking.

I threw down the tenner.

'A blue one, be Jasus,' said Crippen.

'I'll have three coppers out of it,' said MacIntaggart. 'I want to phone my solicitor.'

'A bit early for him, isn't it?' said Cripps.

'Not for this one,' said MacIntaggart, 'he lives in the office.'

'When are you up?'

'Oh, it's a civil action I'm taking against' – here his face set in indignation – 'against the Department of Social Security, against the Relief Officer for neglecting my children . . .'

The Same Again,
Please

Uisce – An Ea?

This is not my first appearance before the Irish public. By no manner of means. Tripping over my musty trusket, or whatever you call it, I made a stand for Ireland at the Mansion House in nineteen thirty-five in a play by the name of *Toirneach Luimnigh**, and had a speaking part of three words, and they may be the best rehearsed three words in the duration of *Feis Átha Cliath** on that or any other stage.

For weeks before, in school and out of it, I tried them with every possible shade of intonation. Just the plain: Listen, give over the mallarkey*, and a straight answer to a straight question, *Uisce, an ea?**

Then the sinister: Little do you know, so you think you double-cross the greatest bandit in all the Mexico, Leo Carillo, the Ceesco Keed, *Eeescha, huh, an ea?*

Or the hurried, efficient violence of Cagney or Edward G. Robinson: C'mon, fishface, 'n come across, accompanied by a slap in the puss with one hand, while the left gripped the forelock, and the victim whimpered: Boss, boss, I didn't did it. Don't gimme that, mugsy, but before your dawgs goes into this bucket of nice fresh cee-ment, uh, uh, or huh, huh, *Uisce, an ea?*

It depended what was on at the Plaza, the Drumcondra Grand, the Bohemian or the Phibsboro for the three months of rehearsal how my style of acting varied, as one form of diction seemed good, till you got another fourpence for the pictures and encountered the next.

On my way across Mountjoy Square to the bakery

in Parnell Street for fourteen outside split loaves for my mother, I'd pass Mrs. Schweppes on the corner, where O'Casey wrote *The Shadow of a Gunman*, and more local loyalties would assert themselves, and I'd return to my naturalistic interpretation of the part: Poor little Mollser, me dollser, and Tommy Owens and Fluther and Captain Boyle, and me bould Jack Clitheroe, yous are toilin' and moilin' and gunnin' and runnin' and fightin' and yous wouldn't help a body out of a hobble and she wriggled in her corporal form be the frightful exertion of an upturned land-mine that she sat down on to rest her poor bones to use towards the holy heights of heaven be the force of the explosion unexpected, listen to me yous, *Uisce, ui-is-ce, an ea?*

At the bakery, I tried them over, and was cursed in the queue for delaying the man.

'Eh, go-be-the-wall, what's that you said you wanted?'

'*Uisce, an ea?*'

'I'm after saying fifteen times there's no turnovers till five o'clock.'

When I'd completed my errand and left the shop with my bag over my shoulder, the crowd looked after me strangely as I muttered my way up Middle Gardiner Street: *Uisce, an ea?*

But the day before the show, my mind was made up for me at the cheek and impudence counter of Hugh MacCallion's shop in Dorset Street. It was said that you paid for the pig's cheek and the impudence was thrown in for choice.

Still, Hugh was a decent old skin in his own way and maybe it was only the uncouth Derry accent that made his utterance so harsh on our refined

Metropolitan ears. No matter what way you looked at it, he was a match for his customers.

This old one asked him for a shilling pig's cheek, and while he muttered about himself paying more than that for them, and all to that effect, the usual old shopman's cant, he was rooting in the barrel for something that he could sell for a shilling and still add something to the Hugh Fund out of it.

At last he emerged from the blood-red depths of the briny barrel bearing aloft the three-quarter profile of a pig, very much battered. It seemed that this cheek had been squeezed up against the side of the barrel by the others and his appearance was certainly very odd.

'There's a grand cheek now for the money,' said Hugh.

The old one looked at it, very doubtfully, and in its twisted way, it returned her glance.

'The Lord between us and all harm, Mr. Hug MacScallion . . . '

'Hugh, Hugh, and my neems MacCallion.'

'Whatever it is, and Hew here or Hew there, that's a very peculiar looking cheek.'

Hugh swelled up bigger than the barrel, looking from her to the cheek as much as to say that if it went to looks there wasn't much between them, and roared: 'An' what do you axpect for a shillin' – Micheál Mac Lallimore?'

I'd seen the noblest youth of the *Fianna** and heard MacLiammóir's high Castilian brogue: *Éist, a chuid den tsaol. Is iad na tonntracha a chanfas amhrán ár bpósta dúinn anocht . . .**

I regretfully decided there would be no excuse accepted for gagging this bit into the Primary Schools

Cup competition, but I could model my interpretation of my part in *Toimeach Luimnigh* on Diarmuid's last words: *Uisce, a Fhinn, tabhair deoch uisce chugam . . .* *

Well, they are not quite the last words. He says at the finish: *Breathnaigh isteach sna súile orm, a Ghráinne.* *

But I didn't think *Feis Átha Cliath* * would wear an interpolation of this nature either, but I'd do the best I could with my head turned sideways till the great moment came.

I was nearly deformed for life, waiting for it. I had to wait, head to one side, like I'd seen your man at the Gate, till the *saighdiúir eile Éireannach* * crouched the far side of me wondered whether there was something offensive about himself or his accoutrements, my head turned away from him for half the play.

A fellow called Pa Bla from that good day to this, though he has since held commissioned rank in the armed forces of this State, comes out in his French uniform, shouting like a Gallic-Gaelic bull: *Parbleu, cad is fiú botún, thall is abhus,* * the significance of which message is forever lost to me, owing to overdue concentration on my twisted neck, so that I might have presented the starboard side of my face when the time came.

A boy from Summerhill called Pigeon is hit by a cannon ball and falls off Limerick's Walls, or whichever of them he was on, before being bombarded by the other crowd, and moans, '*Uisce . . uisce.*'

Up I leaped in my profile. Into bed or out of barracks . . . '*Uisce, an ea?*'

'Sea,' * mutters poor Pigeon.

I see. Nothing like making sure. I'll repeat it.

'Uisce, an ea?'

'Sea, sea.'

I think I was just a little, er, underdone, that time. Besides you can't get too much of a good thing.

'Uisce, an ea?'

'Sea, sea, sea!'

All right. No need to take the needle over it. Just answer a civil question. I walked over, head twisted sideways, to get the water, tripped and nearly broke my neck over a Dutch cavalryman in the wings, and the play went on in my absence.

Pigeon recovered from his cannon ball wound and played professional soccer for Brighton and Hove in England long after the Siege of Limerick.

Red Jam Roll, the Dancer

I am reminded of boxing matters by an encounter I had this day with a former opponent of mine, pugilistically speaking. I do not mean that our encounter this day was a pugilistic one, but it was pugilistically speaking we last spoke. And that, at the lane running alongside the railway end of Croke Park.

Our street was a tough street and the last outpost of toughness you'd meet as you left North Dublin for the red brick respectability of Jones's Road, Fitzroy Avenue, Clonliffe Road, and Drumcondra generally.

Kids from those parts we despised, hated and resented. For the following sins: they lived in houses one to a family which we thought greedy, unnatural

103

and unsocial; they wore suits all the one colour, both jacket and pants, where we wore a jersey and shorts; they carried leather schoolbags where we either had a strap round our books or else a cheap check cloth bag.

Furthermore, it was suspected that some of them took piano lessons and dancing lessons while we of the North Circular Road took anything we could lay our hands on which was not nailed down.

We brought one of them to our corner and bade him continue his performance and thereafter, any time we caught him, he was brought in bondage to the corner of Russell Street and invited to give a performance of the dance: hornpipe, jig, reel, or slip jig.

This young gent, in addition to being caught red-footed, was by colouring of hair red-headed, and I've often heard since that they are an exceedingly bad-tempered class of person which, signs on it, he was no exception. For having escaped from his exercises, by reason of an approaching Civic Guard by name 'Dirty Lug', he ran down to the canal bridge which was the border of our territory and used language the like of which was shocking to anyone from Russell Street and guaranteed to turn thousands grey if they hailed from some other part.

However, our vengeance for the insults heaped upon us by this red-headed hornpiper, that thought so bad of giving the people an old step on the corner of the street, was not an empty one.

One day not alone did we catch him but he'd a jam roll under his oxter – steaming hot, crisp and sweet from the bakery – and the shortest way from Summerhill to where he lived was through our street.

He was tired, no doubt, with wearing suits and living in a house with only his own family and carrying that heavy leather schoolbag, not to mind the dancing lessons; no doubt he thought he had a right to be tired and he took the shortest way home with the cake for his ma.

He could see none of our gang but the fact that he didn't see us didn't mean we were not there. We were, as a matter of fact, playing 'the make in'* on Brennan's Hill down by the Mountjoy Brewery when his approach was signalled by a scout and in short order 'the make in' was postponed while we held up the red fellow and investigated his parcel.

We grabbed the booty and were so intent on devouring the jam roll that we let the prisoner go over the bridge and home to plot his vengeance.

He was a hidden villain all right. Long weeks after, myself and Scoil (or Skull, have it any way you fancy) Kane were moseying round Croker,* not minding anything in particular. Kerry was playing Cavan in Hurling or Derry was playing Tyrone in anything but it wasn't a match of any great import to any save relations and friends, and a dilatory class of a Sunday afternoon was being had by all, when the Scoil (Skull) and myself were surrounded by a gang, if you please, from Jones's Road, and who but the red-headed dancing master at the head of them.

But we didn't take them seriously.

'Sound man, Jam Roll,' said I, not knowing what else to call him.

'I'll give you jam roll in a minute,' said Jam Roll.

'You're a dacent boy,' said I, 'and will you wet the tea as you're at it?'

'Will you stand out?' says Jam Roll.

'I will,' said I.

'In the cod or in the real?'

'The real,' said I, 'd'you take me for a hornpiper?'

He said no more but gave me a belt so that I thought the Hogan Stand had fallen on me. One off the ground. The real Bowery Belt.

'Now,' says he, when I came to, 'you won't call me Jam Roll again.'

'You were wrong there, Jam Roll.'

Belfast was First Right . . . Then Just Straight Ahead

If you went up the North Circular as far as the Big Tree Belfast was on the first turn to the right. Straight ahead. I knew that when I was seven. The country lay out there. I visited it with my grandmother one day she and Lizzie MacKay went out for a breath of air.

After dinner on a Sunday, she put on her black coat and hat and a veil with little black diamonds on it and off we went. We went up the canal from Jones's Road Bridge to Binn's Bridge (and that was nearly in the country already) and into Leech's.

There we sat having a couple till it was shutting and time to get the tram into the real country.

Lizzie and she got a dozen of large bottles and the loan of a basket and we got a currant pan and a half-pound of cooked ham in the shop next door and got on the tram for Whitehall.

'I see yous are well-heeled,' says the conductor, looking at the basket.

'Well, the country, sir,' says my grandmother. 'You'd eat the side wall of a house after it.'

'You're going all the way?'

'To the very end,' says Lizzie MacKay. 'All the way to Whitehall.'

'And I don't suppose that'll be the country much longer,' says the conductor. 'There's houses everywhere now. Out beyond Phibsboro church. They're nearly out to where Lord Norbury disappeared on the way home and the coachman only felt the coach getting lighter on the journey and when he got to the house your man was disappeared and the devil was after claiming him, and good enough for him after the abuse he gave poor Emmet in the dock.'

My grandmother and Lizzie MacKay bowed their heads and muttered, 'Amen.'

'They're nearly out to there,' said the conductor, 'and it won't be long before they're at Whitehall,' giving the bell a bang to hurry the driver up before the builders got there.

We found a fine ditch only a few yards from the end of the tram tracks and nice and handy for getting home, and there was grass and trees over it.

I ran into a field and across a big park till an old fellow with a strawbainer hat started chasing me and cursing till I got out again and ran to my granny and Lizzie.

They sat up in their ditch and took the bottles from their mouths and looked over at the old fellow who was shouting with his red face from the gate.

'Go 'long, you low scruff,' said Lizzie, 'myself and this lady here with the right of being buried in Kilbarrack was here before you were let out of wherever you were let out of. Talking about your park, anyone'd think you owned it!'

The old fellow danced a bit more with temper and

his red face but they waved their bottles at him and he went off.

'Me poor child, you'd want something after that old fellow frightening the little heart out of you. Open another bottle, Lizzie, and give him a bit of ham to take with it.'

We sat on in the setting sun eating and drinking and my grandmother and Lizzie MacKay making remarks about the way the fellows going past were either walking in front of or behind their girls.

'Look at that fellow, Lizzie, swinging his stick, a mile behind the poor one.'

The young man looked over at them, and hurried on to get out of earshot.

'You'd think the poor girl had a contagious disease.'

The man and the girl took one fearful look over at them and fled up the road.

When we got home that night from the country the people asked us where we'd spent the day and my grandmother said we'd been on the Belfast road.

All I had ever heard of Ireland and her green fields and rakes up in rafters and women of three cows *a grá*, was for me situated in north county Dublin and the Belfast road was the golden way to Samarkand.

I learned early on that it was a bit up the road from us that Setanta beat a hurling ball into a dog's mouth and became Cuchulainn.

Out on that road lay Gormanston where my father was locked up and where he saw me for the first time when I was six months old. Seán T.* was in with him and I thought that made Seán T. a fairly important man too.

My cousin who learned more about cattle on the

108

North Circular Road than many a one reared in the Argentine had charge of a big house for some time out Swords direction.

It was a big mansion with an estate and hay barns and cow barns and statues in the gardens. There were about fifty rooms in the main building and a lodge, as Chuckles Malone said, the size of the Bridewell.

People round our way couldn't see anyone lost for a bit of company in a big place like that.

I was brought out for the air and was followed by my father's aunt who wasn't too well. Some of the neighbours brought out a couple more invalids and our team, N.C.R.A.F.C., were in the final of the Conway Cup that year, and they thought it would be a good place to get a bit of training, and with the sick people looking out the windows at the footballers and screaming advice and abuse to young Coughlin to be not so mangy* with the ball, and telling Johnny Foy that he got his head for something else besides keeping his hat on, my cousin said the place was a cross between the Pigeon House Sanatorium and the Fifteen Acres.* There was the best of gas and the life of Reilly to be had by one and all.

And in the summer nights I'd lie in bed and over the noise of the fellows and girls down in the big hall dancing round the coats of armour to the gramophone playing *On Mother Kelly's Doorstep* I'd hear the cars going past and sometimes sneak to the window and follow the noise and the red tail-light till it grew faint and dim going on to the end of the Belfast road through green fields and dusky magic.

To Die without Seeing Dublin!

One of the Michael Dwyer* crowd, whose breed still flourishes round New Street and thereabouts, was back on a visit from the Coombe to the Glen of Imaal, where his grandmother's sister lay dying.

After she was washed and made right for the road the priest sat taking a cup of tea and chatting with her. 'Well, now, and how do you feel, Nan?'

'I feel right enough, now that you've been and settled me; what would be the matter with me? I've known that I was going to die this eighty year past.

'It happened all belonging to me. Though them that does have all the talk about how nice it is in the next world, I don't see any great hurry on them getting on there.'

'I suppose you don't, Nan. But you've no regrets for this one. You reared fine men and women, and saw their rearing up here on the mountain.'

'I have no regret, Father, only the one. I was never in Dublin.'

Sammy Watt in Portrush has the same regret. In his youth there were no paid holidays and now, in ampler times, he's nervous that the Republicans would recognize him and have him shot, maybe lynch him as he walked along O'Connell Street, or tie him to the Bowl of Light place and, as a special *Tóstal** attraction, have him beaten to death with bound volumes of the *Ulster Protestant*.

For Sammy was on the other side in the Tan time.

I had never met anyone who boasted of having fought against the rebels, except the commissionaire of a Liverpool cinema who told me he was in the

Black and Tans and took part in a military operation. This included a raid on a clerical outfitter's in Dame Street.

Suitably garbed, he and his comrades, who had raided a pub or two earlier on, stood in the lorries and blessed the passers-by with upheld Mills grenades.

But the commissionaire only joined up because his girl friend wouldn't leave her work in a tripe factory. And, wanting to forget, he had not got the fare to the Foreign Legion and had to make do with the Black and Tans.

Besides, he thought it was more dangerous, the money was better, and he could help his widowed mother, who was an invalid and could do nothing but sit all day in a bathchair embroidering moral notices, suitable for framing, reading: *Beware!*

'Just the one word', said I, 'and the same one on all the notices?'

'Ah. She weren't much of a speller, my old woman. Nor much of an embroiderer, neither. She weren't bad though, considering the only training she'd ever 'ad was sewing mailbags when she'd be doing a couple of months up in Walton.

'She sent her embroidery all over the world with the missions. You could read *Beware* in my old woman's sewing all over the British Empire. Some places they didn't know enough English, and 'ad to 'ave it explained to them what it was about.

'When I was in your country, forgetting this judy what gave me up for a job in a tripe factory, my old woman, she sent me an embroidering, and it 'ung over the canteen counter – *Beware* – in black and red wool, till the Shinners* let off a landmine.

111

'It blew the roof in on top of the sergeant-major where 'e was 'avin' a pint, and when 'e got over 'is nerves and got up and dusted 'imself, 'e said to take that so-and-so notice off the wall or 'e'd go over to Norris Green and slit my old woman's gizzard, at 'is own expense.'

My commissionaire didn't count, because he wasn't much interested in the rights or wrongs of the war so long as it kept his mind off his troubles.

Sammy spoke with the ardour of the pure-souled and dedicated patriot about his services to King and Empire in those strenuous days.

All my life I've known the opposite convention, where anyone old enough would mutter darkly about their doings and if they weren't in the G.P.O. in 1916 it was because they were doing something more important and to which the element of secrecy was so vital that it hasn't been made public nearly forty years after.

A change is as good as a rest.

'I'm a man that knows what I'm talking about. I was through the whole lot, so Ah was.'

'And what, pray, were you through?' asked his wife, from the far side of the table, 'barrin' it'd be a lock of porter barrels?'

'Och, hould your wheesht, you, Hanna, you knew nawthin' about it, nor was let know. A right thing, if every gabbin' ould woman in the County Derry could be knowing the secrets of the organization.'

'Och, what organization? Filling the wee boy's head up wi' your lies and rubbish.'

I signalled hastily to the barman.

'Port, please, for Mrs. Watt. No, not the Empire, the Portuguese port.'

112

It's not every day in these weeks I get called a 'wee boy'. It might never happen again.

'And a couple of scoops for myself and Sammy.'

We got settled down to his military reminiscences.

'Ah was an Intelligence man.'

'The dear God protect us from the Father of Lies,' muttered Hanna to herself, putting down her glass.

Sammy did not condescend to hear her. 'Yes, Ah was an undercover man like –'

'Dick Barton,' said Hanna.

'Ah was a spy, to tell you straight, though you were on the other side; good men on every side and you're a Fenian; you mind Dave O'Leary?' All in the one breath, and I had to sort it out as best I could.

Fenian Dave O'Leary?

'Would it be John O'Leary, Sammy? He was a Fenian, but he was in the one grave with romantic Ireland a long time before I was born.'

'Och, don't talk daft. This man was in the grave with no one. He stayed out in Portstewart, five mile out the town, only last summer. Isn't he the head one in the Free State? Damn it, sure everyone knows Dave O'Leary.'

'De Valera?'

'Damn it, isn't that who I said? Deyve Ah Leery.'

'Fair enough. What about him?'

'You mind the time he come in Columb's Hall in Derry? Well, Ah goes in, carryin' me life in me hands, among all these Fenians that's packin' the hall out to give him a big cheer when he comes out on the stage to prache.'

'To?'

'To prache the meeting. Ah'm sitting in the sate minding no one and hoping no one will mind me,

113

but I'm in me disguise.'

'What was that,' asked Hanna, 'a temperance pin?'

'I took me hat off, and no one in the place had ever seen the top of me head from the time I got bald, so they didn't know me.

'Till, when Dave O'Leary comes out on the stage there's a big cheer and a roar and the next thing is, the Peelers* is trying to get in the doors and the crowd is baiting them, and Dave O'Leary is away there, up on the stage, and he says that he came to prache, and, begor, he's going to prache, and damn the one will stop him, and in the middle of it I've got down under the seat, and Head Constable Simpson says, "Got you," and he doesn't know me with me bald head till he turns me round and recognizes me from me face, and near drops from surprise.

'"And what and under the dear good God are you doing here, Sammy Watt? D'you think we hadn't enough trouble with the Fenians?"

'"Ah'm an Intelligence man," said I. "A spy."

'"Take yourself to hell out of thon, or I'll spy you, with a kick where it won't blind you." There was me thanks.'

'Ah, sure wasn't it always the way. Look at Parnell.'

'Ah wonder would they hould it again me in Dublin if I snaked down for a wee trip on the *Enterprise?*'

'Couldn't you disguise yourself? Take off your hat until you get back on the train?'

O, Tell Me All About the ... Riots

It was my privilege, at the age of ten years, to march

114

behind the coffin of the veteran Fenian, James Stritch who, I was told afterwards, gave the signal for the boys to attack the van in the famous Manchester Rescue. I saw the late Joe MacGarrity once and damn near plucked up the courage to ask him what he meant by helping to organise the riots against *The Playboy* on the famous Abbey tour of forty odd years ago. For it is his name that appears on the list of bail bondsmen for the *Clann na nGael* drama critics who went in to wreck the show in Philadelphia.

Joe might have told me to go and chase myself or might have said that they weren't going to have the country made a jeer of. If he had, I'd have quoted Padraic Pearse's remarks on censorship to him for Pearse was not of the same mind as Joe MacGarrity on the matter which goes to show that a mutual interest in Irish Independence does not always mean a common taste in literature.

Pearse lifted the censors out of it in a passage, quoted by me in the original Irish, in an article in this newspaper on Saint Patrick's Day last. I shouldn't think in this dear land that everyone would have agreed with it. It must be that the censors don't read Irish or maybe the ones that do don't read THE IRISH PRESS. Of course, they shouted to Cyril Cusack that they didn't understand Irish when he was making his curtain speech in the Gaiety the first night of O'Casey's play.

Be that as it may, I'd have let a few shouts at *The Playboy* myself, on the first night, only for, (i), I wasn't present, and (ii), the play is good gas. For the carry-on of the people on the stage and their old chat is so phoney that no corner-boy in the days of my childhood felt that his repertoire was complete

115

barring he could take off *The Playboy.* 'Oh, man of the roads with your long arm and your strong arm, be after pulling me a pint of porther,' and all to that effect.

The speech is not the speech of native speakers trying to speak English, for that is usually done in an American accent and the idiom of the lower orders of the United States is even prevalent in the Irish itself. I have heard a little girl go into a shop and ask for a *paicéad cáise agus punt** crackers, and another child asked me did I fancy *cereal is bainne** for my breakfast.

Andrew Marvell in his Horatian Ode congratulating Cromwell on his return from Ireland, says:

'And now the Irish are ashamed
To see themselves in one year tamed:
So much one man can do
That does both act and know.'

It is not so much that, but being conquered by such a dull lot of *cawbogues** that couldn't even cook or make good drinks. Now if it had been Napoleon I'd nearly have been in the 'B' Specials.*

The real Playboy, an O'Malley from Erris, was described by Tomás Ó Máille as a 'sturdy, lively young man without being too tall.' If he had been alive in 1919 he'd have been eighty years of age which means he was born sometime around 1840. His father was a man that had a strong weakness for drink, God forgive him, and your man had to leave home and go to sea at an early age.

The Playboy, as we'll call him, sent home money to the father to buy a bit of land which would go to him when he came home from the sea because he was the only son and, anyway, it was bought with his money.

116

He came home in due course, got married, and everything passed off very civil as the man said, till the mother died when lo and behold, the old fellow decides to have another puck off his hurl and get married again himself.

He wouldn't even let our poor Playboy have a little potato garden and one day when he comes out to set a few spuds for himself and the care, the old fellow goes to beat him out of it and starts struggling with him for the loy* till, in the course of combat, the Playboy hits him a belt and the old fellow falls to the ground looking very dead.

Howsomever, he is not altogether gone for his tea, and the women bring him into the house and tell the Playboy not to stall but get himself away as quick as he can. They're not that gone on the old fellow either.

The Playboy goes on the run and spends some time hiding in Connemara – three months if we are to take Tomás Ó Máille literally – 'and it wasn't the place he slept the night he'd be found in the morning but forever on the move as a fugitive, a Tory.'

He went through many adventures the time he was in Connemara hopping over bogs and mountains night and day and often he had to swim a lake to bring his skin with him in one piece. When he was nearly done for, he made his way to the island of Garumna where he got a boat to take him over to Aran. He had relations there, in Kilronan; a girl of the O'Malleys was married into the Hernons. He stayed with them for a while. When the word came that the police were after him there, she had him brought to Inis Meadhon by boatmen of the MacNeela clan – a decent people to this very day as I well know.

He spent a time on Inis Meadhon till the others got the word that he was there and they came over and surrounded the house in the middle of the night. The man of the house told the Playboy to get offside and he would give himself up and pretend he was the man they wanted and when the police came to the door asking for O'Malley, the Playboy opened it for them and said, 'He's inside – take him with you.'

The Playboy shook hands with the man of the house when they brought him off and, by the time the police had found their mistake, he was away and off down to Cork via a potato boat taking a cargo from Aran to Kerry.

He sailed into Galway Harbour years afterwards as a captain of an American steamship unknown to anyone except a few people that had helped him. He treated them well, in their turn, and that was the last known of the Playboy – and that Synge and him and the rioters and actors may get space above to argue it out – a bed in heaven to them all – even the critics.

We Fell into the Waxies' Dargle

'I'm fed up and brassed off,' said Crippen, 'with the Continong.'

'I thought the extent of your travels was to the point of the Wall,' said I. 'When were you on the Continent?'

'I'm gone blue melanconnolly from reading about it. Why can't you write about something natural? Like the time we all fell into the water at the Waxies' Dargle?' *

'Or the time,' said Maria Concepta, 'the slaughterhouse went on fire.'

'Or, the Lord be good to us all,' said Mrs. Brennan, 'the time the holy chap told us the end of the world was come to Dún Laoghaire and we were all going to meet a watery end at the butt end of the East Pier.'

'It's like the time,' said Maria Concepta, 'we seen the film about the king and all the people stood up.'

'I'd have stood up for no king,' said Crippen crossly.

'You would,' said Mrs. Brennan, 'if you'd have seen this one.'

'He was masterful,' said Maria Concepta, 'like me first husband who was only five foot nothing but very stern.'

'Maria Concepta,' said Mrs. Brennan, 'give us that little stave about the Waxies' Dargle.'

'Well', said Maria Concepta, 'I'm not as good as I was the time I took first place and silver medal at the Fish Coyle.'*

'Ah, poor ould Fish,' said Mrs. Brennan, 'he wasn't bad when he had it.'

'Well,' said Crippen, 'give us the stave.'

'I will so,' said Maria Concepta, making a noise like a cinder under a gate.

> 'Oh, says my ould one to your ould one,
> "Will you come to the Waxies' Dargle?"
> And says your ould one to my ould one,
> "Sure I haven't got a farthing . . . "'

'God love your stomach,' said Crippen.

'Ahmen, O Lord,' said Mrs. Brennan, with feeling.

'Thank yous, dear faithful follyers,' murmured Maria Concepta. 'It may be the last time I'll be singing at yous.'

'Thank *you*,' said Crippen . . . *"But there's them that*

says the divil is dead . . . "

'Not half sooing enough,' said Mrs. Brennan, 'to hell with him.'

> 'And there's more that says he's hearty
> And some says that he's down below
> Eating sugary barley . . . '

Maria Concepta finished on a low and throbbing note.

'That was massive,' said Mrs. Brennan.

'Not a diver in the Port and Docks could have got under that,' said Crippen.

'I would like, as you're the most melodious mezzo-soprano that ever muffled the markets,' said Mrs. Brennan, 'if you'd condescend to give us a verse of the *Zozzoligcal Gardings.*'

'Ah, the dear old days,' said Maria Concepta.

'Quite right,' said Mrs. Brennan, explaining, 'we both met our husbands in the Zoo.'

'Quite right, ma'am, and damn the lie,' said Maria Concepta, 'myself and my poor fellow' – she choked from emotion – 'we met in the monkey house. And shared a bag of nuts with an orang-outang.'

'Well, carry on with the coffing, the corpse'll walk,' said Crippen, jovially, 'give us that bit of a bar.'

'I will so and the divil thank the begrudgers,' said Maria Concepta, 'with no more ahdo,' and without further ado she broke into a croak:

> 'I brought me mot up to the Zoo
> For to show her the lion and the kangaroo,
> There were he-males and she-males of each
>   shade and hue
> Inside the Zoological Gardens . . .'

'My poor ould uncle – oney . . . '

'Owney?' I asked.

'Oney a marriage relayshing,' went on Mrs.

120

Brennan. 'He used to sing that. Till they buried him – after he died – in Kilbarrack. Out be Howth direction. That cementery is so healthy for dead people that if a live one had have went out there, they'd be there yet, and going on for all time, meeting themselves coming back.'

Paris – Visit it only in the Spring

'Some day maybe I'll go back to Paris
And welcome in the dawn at Chatelet
With onion soup and rum to keep us
    nourished
Till the sun comes up on St. Germain de
    Pres ...'

And, as the man said, it wouldn't be the first time. This is the time of the year for it. In the winter, Paris is habitable by brass monkeys and, in the summer, you'd die for a breath of the sea. That's when people from here learn to appreciate our situation. A shilling will take you to the Bull Wall or the Forty Foot but, in the heat of the Paris summer, it'll cost you two shillings to go into the *Piscine* which is a sort of floating swimming pool on the Seine. For one hour only. They control the length of time by a system of coloured tickets and when they shout out that it's time up for the yellow tickets or the blue tickets it's no good gaming on that you don't know what *jaune* or *bleu* means.

You can't stop there till it shuts and they'll charge you the difference afterwards – like travelling first class on a third class Metro ticket. The inspector, if he catches you, will waste no time bemoaning the dishonesty of any part of the human race, yours or his. He'll hold out his hand for a ten-shilling fine.

And once, at a party held on a little island, under the auspices of some students from Trinity College, Dublin, I dived in from the Pont Notre Dame. The *pompiers*, or river fire brigade, shone searchlights from their boats.

I hardly had my clothes on when the *flic* were down wanting to know what I thought I was making of the place altogether and where I was from and had I my papers? I showed them my papers and they saw the cover of the passport and bothered me no more. One nodded to the other not to mind me, that I was an Irishman, and tapped the side of his cap to indicate that I was one of the Gormans of Grange and a foreman in the puzzle factory.

He saluted and wished me a civil good-night and they went off, much gratified, to the strains of *The Marseillaise* sung by the choir of Trinity scholars in the version attributed to its distinguished alumnus known as The Pope:

'Oh, the Board takes grave excep - chi -
o - on, . . .
yours sincerely, Matty Fry . . . '

As the Paris police are mentioned, let me say this much about them. Some people from the island across the way and Irish visitors from that stratum of society that would eat cooked Kenyan if they thought the Quality over the way were doing likewise adversely criticise them as armed State police as compared to the dear old village constable in Dryraching-under-the-water.

My grandmother's favourite toast was: 'Here's to the harp of old Ireland and may it never want for a string as long as there's a gut in a Peeler,' and I am not that mad about police of any sort myself but my experience of the Paris police has been a pleasant one.

In a spirit, quite in keeping with the democratic tradition of their country, they will reprimand the wealthy *rentier* in his *delage* and the workman carrying his child on the back-wheel and as freely assist them. French or foreign, rich or poor, they are at everyone's disposal and, if your papers are right, they don't care how little else you have in your pocket; you can go on home and the sleep will do you good.

The best spot from which to view the chestnuts and beautiful Paris in the spring is the top of the Arc de Triomphe. I was up there, like any other tourist, and worse is to come, a true born Dubliner: *I have been on top of the Pillar.*

I first noticed the Pillar, one day not long ago, when I met a man, a pal of my cradle days. We graduated together to the more serious considerations of 'the make in,' 'fat,' 'pontoon,' and the 'ha'penny rummy'*, before emigration parted us. He went to the Navan end of Cabra and Paw and Maw and us broke virgin soil in the highlands of Kimmage.

I came out of Henry Street and who should I see but my old school mate staring up at the top of the Pillar before.

'Me tearing man, Jowls. I didn't know you were out.'

'Aw hello the hard. Yes, this three weeks. Wasn't bad, I was in the laundry during the winter.'

He was still examining your man on the Pillar as

123

closely as he could from a distance of a hundred feet.

'Very interesting that. Up there.'

'Nothing got to do with us.'

He looked at me angrily.

'Why hasn't it got something to do with us?'

I had never suspected such loyalty in the bosom of the Jowls who sat with me, a boy, under the watchful eye of the French Sisters of Charity in the North William Gaeltacht.*

'Did you ever go up and look at him?'

I started off the usual long spiel about being a Dublin man, but Jowls cut me short.

'Come on up, and I'll show you. It'll give us an appetite for a couple.'

We started in and, to cut a long story short, I died seven deaths on the way up, all from shortness of breath. Jowls was in better condition being just back to this sinful world from his place of retirement. We got up to the top and I crawled out after him to the platform, or whatever you call it, and knelt before Nelson. I hadn't the strength to stand.

Jowls looked up at the Hero of Trafalgar, sighed deeply, and reached up to pat the sword, victorious shield of England, home and beauty. I looked up at Jowls and said humbly, 'Napoleon wasn't a bad one either.'

He came out of his reverie, 'Wha'? Do you see that?' He tapped the point of the sword. I nodded up to him.

'D'you know what I'm going to tell you, there's about a fiver's worth of scrap in that. It's not much but not much trouble either, of a dark evening, and bring it down wrapped up in brown paper; they'd never miss it till morning.'

The Tale of Genockey's Motor Car

'It's not every day in the week I get invited to an eviction,' said I.

'It's not an eviction,' said Dion. 'Only a seizure of the goods, as heretofore mentioned. One Chrysler motor car on which there are twelve instalments owing to the Farmers and Merchants Heart and Hand United Mutual Assistance Company (Incorporated in Great Britain).

'I'm owed nothing. My commission came out of the first advance from the Farmers and Merchants, God bless them,' he added cheerfully. 'I'm only there to identify the goods. We're meeting Mr. Claythorpe of the Farmers and Merchants at the premises of Mr. Genockey, the purchaser of the Chrysler car, aforesaid. Mr. Carr here – very appropriate name – is going to seize the car, or what's left of it, and give it over to Mr. Claythorpe.

'I'm there to identify the goods and renew acquaintance with Mr. Genockey who has, in the transaction, benefitted me to the extent of some scores of pounds and is, in my opinion, one of the most remarkable men of our time. If you ask my opinion, he's a credit to his country and the sort of man that Ireland wants. Mr. Carr, as a Sheriff's man of some antiquity...'

'Fifty year, and only off suspended once over me little trouble.' Mr. Carr is a small man, wearing a black suit with little lapels and drainpipe trousers like a Teddy Boy gone backwards and with an old pair of eyes, God bless the mark, that look as if he's got them in a forced sale. 'And though I won't go as far as to

125

agree with Dionysius about Mr. Genockey, the defaulter in the present case, as to say that he is a credit to his country, I will say he keeps us Sheriff's men going. It's only a year or so since the case of the washing machine.'

'This Mr. Genockey,' said Dion, driving North from Lower Mount Street, 'hires a washing machine, pays one down payment but no more and, after hiring it out to every old one in the neighbourhood at three bob an hour *and* pay for the juice for two years, they finally got round to seizing it. You were there, Mr. Carr?'

'Yes, Dionysius, it was one of my cases. He got it as a birthday present for his wife, wrote his name in Irish on the order form. That's how they didn't twig him.

'They asked him how his name in Irish was spelt differently before and he said there was different kinds of Irish and he believed in giving them all a go, a fair field and no favour, "Up Down" and every man for his own county.

'The hire purchase man cried when he saw the state of the washing machine but Mr. Genockey told him to cheer him up, so to speak, that it was only where he'd lent it to a man to mix concrete in, a neighbour was putting down a bit of a path in the garden.'

We pulled up at the premises aforesaid, beside an expensive looking black Humber. An expensive looking gentleman with a moustache got out of it and stood with us on the pavement.

'Good afternoon, Mr. Claythorpe,' said Dion.

'Effanoon, 'm,' said Mr. Claythorpe from between his cool, white teeth and, nodding to Mr. Carr, 'Effanoon, Cur.'

'Good afternoon, sir,' moaned Mr. Carr respect-
fully.

Mr. Claythorpe looked at me. 'You a bailiff's man?'

'He's a newsboy,' said Mr. Carr. 'He's only here
with Dion, sir.'

'Well, I suppose we had better go in, Cur,' said
Claythorpe.

We were met by a smiling big woman with a
Munster accent.

'Yeer the man that's coming to see Mr. Genockey
about the oul' car? Come in and rest yourselves a
minute. Is that yourself, Mr. Carr? Friends meet
though the hills and the mountains doesn't. I didn't
see you now, Mr. Carr, not since the washing
machine, and God help you, it must have been an
awful trouble to you carrying it down the stairs and
you sit down, sir,' she said to Mr. Claythorpe, 'you're
another friend of Mr. Genockey's.'

'May neem is Claythorpe,' said Mr. Claythorpe
through clenched teeth.

'Ah sure himself'd murder me if I let you out of the
house before he comes back. It's often he does be
talking about you. He won't be long. He's only gone
in the oul' car to Athlone to bring back a few pigs. He
brought down a load of coal in it to oblige the man
he's buying the pigs off. He said he'd be back at three
o'clock to the dot though the oul' car might have
broken down, it's only a heap of scrap now, but sure
nothing lasts only for a time, ourselves included,' –
she put her hand to her ear – 'now here he is.'

Mr. Genockey came into the room, kissed his wife,
and shook hands with Mr. Carr and Dion, 'How's
every bit of yous?' He looked at me and smiled, 'You
the Sheriff? I'm like a big kid I am, I'd love to meet

127

the Sheriff. Have you your star? And your six-gun?"

Mr. Claythorpe spoke from behind him, his face pale and his knuckles showing white where he gripped the back of a chair. He struggled to get out the hoarse words, 'Genockey! I'm Claythorpe!'

Mr. Genockey turned. 'Well, I'm more nor pleased to meet you in the flesh,' he smiled affectionately, 'though we're a kind of pen pals, we still only know each other by correspondence. *Acushla,** did you make Mr. Claythorpe a cup of tea?'

Mr. Claythorpe looked as if he could do with it.

'The old car is outside and you can have it with a heart and a half as soon as I get the few pigs out of it.'

Later, I asked Dion, what was Mr. Carr's little trouble that got him suspended from his office.

'He discovered a law that said that all pawnbrokers that hadn't attended Divine Service the previous Sabbath had to pay a fine of seven-and-sixpence, and he went round collecting it and charging an extra half-a-crown for lip when they were slow to pay up.'

Three Celtic Pillars of Charity

This life is full of disappointments. The band of the Beaux Arts School is one of them. Not in noise, volume or variety of costume but, as the man said, basically.

The Ecole des Beaux Arts, or the the School of Fine Arts in Paris in the popular imagination, is a sort of *Tír na nÓg** of young geniuses, painting and sculpting with fresh, savage efficiency during the working day, cursing the professors, damning all academics, till the light fades, the stars rise over the garret, and Mimi, the little *midinette*, knocks timidly on the door and comes in with the bottle of wine, the piece of veal, the garlic, the bread and cheese purchased, mayhap, with the fruits of her long day's stitching for the rude and haughty ladies of the rue de Faubourg Saint Honoré.

And if, at festival time, he dashes madly through the streets most daring of his band, well, youth must have its fling, and the staid conventions of looking where you are going are not for such ardent spirits as these.

The present Beaux Arts School has a band. Its instruments are not the usual instruments of brass and reed; they are composed mostly of household instruments.

During the summer nights they have a march-out at least every Saturday night, up and round the narrow streets of the Latin Quarter, playing in close harmony on buckets, tin cans, biscuit tins, old motor horns, auctioneers' hand bells, basins, bowls, with a male and female voice choir in sections variously represented; the howl, the screech, the moan, the groan, the roar, the bawl, the yell, the scream, the snarl, the bay, the bark, in time to the steady and rhythmic thud of the big bass dust-bin, and the more sombre tones of the tin-bath.

Along the street the foreigners smiled and nodded indulgently at each other. Dear old Paris. Dear old Latin Quarter has never changed since Mimi's hand was frozen; since Gene Kelly's feet were hot; since the last time we were over.

We wondered at the sour looks on the faces of the French and the disgruntled voice of the big vegetable porter who cursed the noise and said people had to be up at five in the morning to go to work.

Don't bother with work we thought; those lads outside aren't worried about work. Free spirits. Another cognac there, *garçon*; the noise did not upset us. This is what we came to Paris for. Outside they were advancing on Saint Germain. Someone beat the bath on the boulevard.

I turned to Donal and, amidst the satisfied sighs of the foreigners and the curses of the French, shook my head indulgently, and remarked apropos the vegetable porter and other native grumblers: 'Woe to the begrudgers. Aren't they gas men, the art students? *Is maith an rud an óige.*'

'They manage an imitation of it,' a voice beside me said.

I turned and saw that a girl had come in and was standing beside us.

'What does who manage an imitation of?' I asked.

'You said in Irish that youth is a great thing. You were obviously referring to those dreary architects making a nuisance of themselves up the street.'

'What architects? Anyway how did you know what I said in Irish?'

'I suppose I went to school as much as you did.'

'That'd be small trouble to you. But what architects are you talking about?'

'Those fellows going around the place doing the hard chaw, keeping everybody awake. You, like all the tourists –'

I choked with indignation and my fellow-travellers, an American textile foreman, a Scots honeymoon couple and two London schoolmasters, gazed at her with disgust. The foul word that had just left her lips stamped her in all our eyes as a cad or a caddess. It's not a word used in polite society along the boulevards unless you are speaking of somebody else, of course.

She went on relentlessly.

'You people think it's all very romantic but those little architectural students, as soon as they qualify, buy a nice suit, grow a moustache, and refer to this period as the time they were sowing their wild oats.

'I wouldn't mind but I've got to get up and go over to Neuilly and be at the church of Saint Pierre in the morning.'

'Tomorrow is not Sunday,' said Donal. 'Is it a holy day over here?'

'Maybe it's a wedding you're going to,' said I. 'Have another citronade on the head of it.'

'No, thanks. I'm for bed. It's not a wedding I'm going to. I'm going to work. Some people do, you know. I leave my tools here on my way from the school and Madame is just gone to collect them. Ah, here she is.'

She beamed back at the fat old *patronne* whose face for the first time since I'd seen her was split in a smile as she handed over the counter what looked like a kit of tools belonging to a bricklayer.

'*Merci, madame.*'

The old one smiled again. That's twice in the one twenty-four hours.

'*Service, Madamoiselle Murfee.*'

Mlle. Murphy said good night to us too and went off up the rue Dauphine, a trim slip of a girl, as they say at home, but swinging her hammers and chisels with an air.

The church of Saint Pierre is the parish church of Neuilly in south-west Paris. It is about the size of the

131

Dublin Pro-Cathedral and is nearly a hundred years old, no older than the University Church on Dublin's Green, and as beautiful in a different style.

Like Chartres, Bruges, towering and mighty, since the age of Faith, this modest and middle-age suburban church was decorated by a group of sculptors, unpaid, and giving themselves, mind and muscle, for God's sake.

The parish priest of Saint Pierre had about enough money to keep the church in repair, to pay a couple of charwomen and a verger. He had nothing over for ornamentation, for the lovely stone that practically shouted for a chisel.

God's help, they say in Irish, is never further than the door; in this case, the door of the Ecole des Beaux Arts.

Someone in the school heard of all this lovely stone going unadorned and the next thing a squad of students are out, fighting to divide the church up amongst them.

Kathleen Murphy, of Ballymore Eustace, comes away with three pillars and with hammer upraised, poises her slim self to strike a blow *do chum glóire Dé agus onóra na hÉireann.* *

These pillars represent in their tortuous Celtic way the struggle of Christian France against the Huns, the Creation and the Deluge. Standing there, in the quiet of the Avenue de Roule, in the Church of Saint Pierre, the noise of the traffic round the Etoile and on the Champs Elysées dim in the distance, I noted lovingly the twisted features of each cantankerous countenance, thought of Raphoe, Cashel, Clonmacnoise, and heard the waves of the Atlantic break on the Aran shore and the praising voice of the holy Irish, long since dead, soft in the gathering dusk.

A Turn for a Neighbour

One Christmas Eve, though not this one nor the
one before, there was a man coming in from
Cloghran, County Dublin, on a horse and cart to do
his Christmas business, selling and buying.

When he got as far as Santry, County Dublin, he
remembered that there was an old neighbour dead in
a house, so he went in to pay his respects and, after
saying that he was sorry for their trouble and all to
that effect, he enquired whether he could offer any
assistance of a practical nature.

'Well, if it's a thing you wouldn't mind, collecting
the coffin; it's ready-measured and made and all; it
would be a great help to us.'

'I do not indeed mind carrying the coffin back for
you, though I won't be home till a bit late, having to
do her shopping. I've a list as long as your arm, of
sweets for children, snuff for her old one, rich cake, a
jar of malt, two bottles of port wine, snuff for my old
one, a collar for the dog, a big red candle to put in the
window, a jockey of tobacco for myself, a firkin of
porter, two dolls that'll say Ma-Ma, one railway train,
a jack-in-the-box and a monkey-on-a-stick, two holy
pictures, rashers, and black and white pudding and
various other combustibles too numerous to mention.

'But I'll stick the coffin up amongst the rest of
them and take the height of good care of it and it'll be
me Christmas box and hansel for me poor old
neighbour and a good turn for myself because I'll

have luck with it.'

So off he went at a jog-trot into the city down from
Santry, County Dublin, past Ellenfield and Larkhill,
through the big high trees, and the sun just beginning
on a feeble attempt to come out, and then having a
look at the weather it was in, losing heart, and going
back in again, till your man came to Whitehall tram
terminus, where they were just getting ready to take
the seven o'clock into town.

'Morra, Mick,' shouts a tram fellow, with his
mouth full of steam, 'and how's the form?'

'If it was any better,' shouts Mick off the cart, 'I
couldn't stick it.'

'More of that to you,' shouts the tram fellow, 'and
a happy Christmas, what's more.'

'You, too, and many more along with that,' shouts
Mick, and along with him down the Drumcondra
Road.

So away he goes into the city, over Binn's Bridge,
and into the markets. Before dinner-time he had his
selling done and was on to the buying.

He had a good few places to visit, meeting this one
and that, but with an odd adjournment he had
everything bought and the coffin collected and on
the back of the cart with the rest of the stuff by
evening-time. It was dark and cold and the snow
starting to come down the back of his neck, but he
tightened the collar well round him, and having
plenty of the right stuff inside him began a bar of a
song for himself, to the tune of *Haste to the Wedding*:

"Twas beyond at Mick Reddin's, at Owen
     Doyle's weddin,
The lads got the pair of us out for a reel,
Says I, "Boys, excuse us," says they, "don't

134

refuse us,"
"I'll play nice and aisy," said Larry O'Neill.

Then up we got leppin' it, kickin' and
    steppin' it,
Herself and myself on the back of the door,
Till Molly, God bless her, fell into the dresser,
And I tumbled over a child on the floor.

'Says herself to myself, "You're as good as the
    rest,"
Says myself to herself, "Sure you're better nor
    gold."
Says herself to myself, "We're as good as the
    best of them,"
"Girl," says I, "sure we're time enough old."'

So, with a bit of a song and a mutter of encouragement to the old horse, Mick shortened the way for
himself, through snow and dark, till he came to
Santry, County Dublin, once again.

There was light and smoke and the sound of
glasses and some fellow singing the song of *The Bould
Tenant Farmer* and Mick, being only human, decided
to make one last call and pay his respects to the
publican.

But getting in was a bit easier than getting out, with
drinks coming up from a crowd that was over from
the other side of the county, all Doyles, from the hill
of Kilmashogue, the Drummer Doyle, the Dandy
Doyle, Jowls Doyle, Woodener Doyle, the Dancer
Doyle, Elbow Doyle, Altarboy Doyle, the Hatchet
Doyle, Coddle Doyle, the Rebel Doyle, Uncle Doyle,
the Shepherd Doyle, Hurrah Doyle and Porternose

Doyle.

There was singing and wound opening, and citizens dying for their country on all sides, and who shot the nigger on the Naas Road, and I'm the first man that stuck a monkey in a dustbin and came out without a scratch and there's a man there will prove it, that the lie may choke me, and me country's up and me blood is in me knuckles. 'I don't care a curse now for you, or your queen, but I'll stand by my colour, the harp and the green.'

Till by the time he got on the road again Mick was *maith go leor*,* as the man said, but everything went well till he was getting near Cloghran and he had a look round, and there he noticed – the coffin was gone! Gone like Lord Norbury with the divil, as the man said.

Ah, what could he do at all, at all? He sat on the cart for a minute and wondered how he'd face your man if he had to go and tell him that he'd let him down not doing the turn for a family with enough of trouble this Christmas Eve.

Still, looking at it never fattened the pig, so he got off and went back along the road in the direction of the city, and was moseying round in the snow when an R.I.C.* man came up from Santry Barracks.

'Come on you, now, and what are you doing walking round this hour of the night?'

'I'm after losing a coffin, Constable,' says Mick.

'They sells desperate bad stuff this time of the year,' sighs the policeman, taking Mick by the arm. 'Come on, my good man, you'll have to come down the road with me now till we instigate investigations into your moves.'

Poor Mick was too disheartened even to resist

him, and, sad and sober, he trudged through the
snow till they came to the barracks. They went into
the dayroom and the constable said to the sergeant,
'I've a fellow here, wandering abroad, and says he's
after losing a coffin.'

'He may well have,' says the sergeant, 'because
we're after finding one. There it is, standing up
behind the door.'

They looked round and Mick's face lit up with joy
and relief. 'Praise Him,' said he, running over and
throwing his arms round it, 'there it is, me lovely
coffin.'

He explained all about it and they let him go off
carrying it back to the cart.

'Take better care of it, now,' says the constable and
the sergeant from the door.

'I wouldn't have minded,' says Mick, 'only this
coffin is not my own. Good night and a happy
Christmas to you, and to everyone.'

We Crossed the Border

My mother had two husbands – not at the one
time of course. She married the first a little time
before Easter Week, 1916, and spent her honeymoon
carrying messages for her husband, brother, brothers-
in-law, and generally running round with my aunts
and her sisters in misfortune shifting one another's
dumps and minding one another's babies for a long
time afterwards.

The peaceful Quaker man that founded the business would be very surprised that, with the Post Office
where Uncle Joe was, and Marrowbone Lane where

Uncle Mick was, his biscuit factory was to my childhood a blazing defiance of Mausers, uncles and my step-brothers' father, against

> ' ... odds of ten to one,
> And through our lines they could not pass
> For all their heavy guns,
> They'd cannon and they'd cavalry,
> Machine-guns in galore,
> Still, it wasn't our fault that e'er a one
> Got back to England's shore ... '

Give over, before I hit a polisman!

Belfast figures as the refuge in cosy remoteness and peace, after the battle had ended and the hunt left behind, because it was there my mother had her first home and her husband had his first job after the Rising.*

It was there that she began her married life and, after the guns and the bombs and the executions, began a stock of more homely domestic anecdotes, like the time she tried him with a curried stew and he ran to the tap after tasting it wondering why she was trying to poison him.

They weren't the only refugees either. A former Captain of the Guard at Leinster House is remembered with indignation for coming in amongst the twenty or thirty people assembled in close formation for the Sunday night *scoraíocht** and remarking through the haze of Irish tobacco smoke that the place was like an oven.

And after Rory was christened Roger Casement in the church, my Uncle Peadar, a sort of walking battery of Fenianism, held him in his arms on Cave Hill and, with the baby's father acting as sponsor, swore him into the I.R.B.*

The little house in the Mount became a clearing house for the Dublin crowd to and from Liverpool and Glasgow.

And to this day, my mother remembers the kindness of the neighbours. Their great interest was the baby Fenian though, being respectable and polite, they never referred to his politics nor to the comings and goings and up-country accents of the young men visiting the house at all hours of the day and night.

There might be a satisfied remark about the larruping the Germans were getting on the Somme, but when the Peelers came nosing round the quarter, it was the widow of a Worshipful Master came up with the wind of the word.

'There was polis round here this morning, ma'm, enquiring about some people might be hiding from the military in Dublin. Rebels, if you please. Round here!

'Sure as we all said it's an insult to a loyal street to think the like, Rebels, Sinn Féiners,* hiding round here. And how's our wee man the day? Did you do what I said about the . . . '

My first visit to the North or for the matter of that to any part of Ireland outside Dublin took me to Newry with a train-load of soccer players, accordionists, corkscrew operatives, the entire production under the masterly direction of my Uncle Richie.

He was a non-military uncle and, indeed, had been accused of only remembering the significance of Easter Monday, 1916, by reference to a gold watch, his possession of which dated from that time.

Another souvenir of the six days was a pair of fur-lined boots which were worn out by my time, though they still hung in their old age under the picture of Robert Emmet and 'Greetings for Christmas and a Prosperous 1912' card from 'Dan Lehan, the Patriotic Sand Dancer and Irish National Coon. Performed Soft Shoe before the Crowned Heads of Europe, also Annual Concerts, Mountjoy and the Deaf and Dumb Institution.'

When Uncle Richie had a sup up, he'd fondle the old fur boots and looking from Robert Emmet to the Irish National Coon remark, 'By God, there was men in Ireland them times.'

When the other Jacobs' and G.P.O. uncles were hard at it, remembering the sudden death of a comrade, Uncle Richie shook his head with the rest.

'When you think of what they did to poor Brian, poor pig. Cut the two legs of the man. Them Danes.'

Gritting his teeth and controlling his temper, looking round the room, and a good job for the Danes there weren't any of them knocking around our way.

He wasn't really my uncle at all but a far out relative in another branch of our family, one of our family from around north and east Dublin.

Mostly he didn't bother much about the cause or old Ireland or any of that carrying on. When he was bent in thought it wasn't the declining Gaeltacht was knotting his brow nor the lost green field, but we respected it just the same.

He sat in the corner and looked the same way as our uncle remembering the time they met John Devoy or killed one another during the Civil War. But we knew that this deep cogitation meant that Uncle Richie was thinking up a stroke.

His final stroke brought me to Newry. He hired an

excursion train for a deposit of thirty shillings and our team went up to play a team representing the Ancient Order of Hibernians.

In consideration of his putting up a set of solid silver medals for the contest Uncle Richie's nominee was allowed to take half the gate, and he collected the ticket money from the people on the understanding that he would bring it to the G.N.R.* on Monday morning and receive a small percentage for his trouble.

The whole street saved up for a while and the train was packed with old ones, young ones, singers and dancers, on the way up.

Uncle Richie got the team in a corner and swore that by this and that they had to win those medals and he seemed very serious about it.

Someone asked who were the Ancient Order of Hibernians and was told they were a crowd that carried pikes and someone else said they'd lodge an objection that you wouldn't see the like of that with Merville and Bendigo in the Fifteen Acres.

The Ancient Order of Hibernians had no pikes but, before half-time, they could have done with them. They were all over our crowd in everything except dirt. The double tap, the hack, the trip, the one-two and every manner of lowness, but to no avail. The A.O.H. won 2-nil.

Uncle Richie had to hand over the set of medals and, though he wasn't a mean man, you could see he felt it.

He muttered to Chuckles Malone to get us down to the station quickly and lock the doors. He wouldn't be long after us.

Neither he wasn't, as the man said. But came

running down towards us with half the town after him and they shouting and cursing about the medals. Someone said they weren't bad medals considering they were made out of the tops of milk bottles.

The crowd were in full cry after Uncle Richie, but gaining little. We shouted encouragement to him, 'Come on, Uncle Richie, come on, ye boy ye,' till at last he fell against the gate of the Residency and we hauled him on in the nick of time from the berserk natives.

Carrie Swaine, a Plymouth Sister from Ballybough, called out in triumph, 'Go 'long, yous Orange --s,' which for some reason drove the Ancient Order of Hibernians A.F.C. to a very dervish dance of fury.

Past Clontarf Station Carrie smelt the Sloblands and, from an excess of emotion, shouting 'Law-villy Dublin,' put her head through the window without taking the trouble to lower it and nearly decapitated herself.

Uncle Richie gave a big night in the club and was seen off by the whole street to the Liverpool boat. He expressed no bitterness against the town of Newry or the inhabitants except to remark that the medals were waterproof.

I don't know what he told the railway company.

Orange was Green

It's a source of chronic surprise to me that when you come to the actual Border there is no white line. My childhood idea persists that it should be marked out like a football pitch, even after I've seen a couple of *real* borders. I mean borders *between* countries, not *across* them.

It's the custom of the Automobile Association to mark the county boundaries in Irish and English in the Twenty-six Counties, but in English only in the Six.

The sign on the boundary of Armagh and Louth announces 'Co. Armagh' on the Louth side and 'Co. Lughbhaidh' on the Six-county side of the sign. The Dungiven committee must be asleep on the job. *Séimhiús* and *síneadh fadas** looking in at them all along the Border.

Once inside it, the most interesting thing to an old southern gentleman like myself is the sight of a band of punters inside an office, just as you'd see in any bookie's shop in Summerhill or the Coombe. Sharp-featured men with *The Sporting Chron* well creased and a fair idea of what's in Jarvis's mind to-day.

Elderly females with shopping bags and the usual old man, there's a great supply of them, scrooging his way with muttered imprecations to examine the racing sheet through an enormous eye-glass that looks like it fell out of a searchlight.

I feel sure that an examiner could have tested their knowledge of the Catechism with a shouted question, 'What is Brother Cliff for Sir Gordon to-day at Haydock Park?'* and he confident of the answer, reverently intoned, 'An efficient deputy' and perhaps, a whispered 'we hope' from a weaker vessel let down for a three cross double the day before that.

I travelled to Banbridge with a man from the Co. Down coast. He was from Killough direction. I remembered Saint John's Point and the little ruined church and how I discovered that Unionists have feelings.

143

Along the coast were the survivors of the old stock, in little houses and on bits of rocky land stretching all the way to Slieve Donard.

Harry Loughrey, turned twenty and just off a trip to the River Plate, swam with me every day off the rocks and we roaring like sea-lions in the water. He was teaching me *The Wedding Samba* in Spanish in return for my Uncle Peadar's *Fenian Men* in Irish:

> 'Is é rud atá ráite nar éirigh an cás leo,
> Ach an bás, ba é sin an t-aon rud bhí i ndán
> dóibh,
> Ach, ba bheag leo an bás, agus Éire ina
> náisiún ... '*

We went down the road and saw a crowd round the old chapel of Saint John. They were a historical or archaeological society out for the day. They stood round in their tweed costumes and linen jackets while a gentle-looking old man in knickerbockers talked about the district and the old chapel being the oldest place of Christian worship in Ireland.

We came up, swinging our togs and towels, and they smiled a welcome and made room for us nearer the speaker, as much as to say, 'Come right in, you're welcome, glad to see you taking an interest.'

The old man spoke about the history of the area and the meaning and origin of the place-names and when he was finished he spoke to Harry and me and he seemed delighted to know that Harry's mother was an O' this and his granny a Mac the other.

He talked about Dublin to me and asked me how I liked Co. Down. I said I liked it well and for the want of something to say remarked on the way the little ruin was looked after. There was a fence in good repair around it and a notice to tell you where to find the caretaker.

'But of course,' he smiled, 'it's well looked after. It's a national monument.'

'You mean *you* recognise it as a national . . . '

The smile faded sadly from his face.

'I mean the Northern . . . I mean the government . . . '

I mean that I wished the ground would open and swallow me like the Tuatha de Danaan* or the Firbolgs* or whoever *we* chased out of it.

'Yes,' he said wistfully, 'I suppose it's a fair question. I'm a Planter by origin and a Unionist by politics. So I think are all of us here.' He smiled again.

'Well, I suppose, we had better be getting along for lunch. Goodbye, boys.'

His company suited its pace to his old man's walk but he was gone over the hill before I remembered that my great-great-great grandfather, who came from the North quays to work on the new Royal Canal, was named Banks, Tom Banks. He was a lock-keeper between Binn's Bridge and Cross Guns and got his son into the Four Courts, a place you wouldn't find many Milesians* those times, even running messages for the doormen.

'Well, here we are at Banbridge,' said my Killough friend.

We went in and had a couple to ease the parting and I went over to examine the memorial while I waited for the bus. The stone man at the bus stop had hard earned his bit of respect.

'Although, there remained no survivors of the expedition, enough has been ascertained to shew that to it is justly due the honour of the discovery of the long sought *North West Passage*, and that Captain Crozier, having survived his chief, perished with the remainder of the party, after he led them to the coast of America.

'He was born at Banbridge, the tenth of September, 1796, but of the place or time of his death, no man knoweth.'

Turnip Boat

For some reason a friend of mine wanted to ship turnips from a Six Counties' port. He wanted to ship anything from a Six Counties' port because he wanted to sail into a British port with a British Customs manifest, or whatever Mac Lir would call it.

Our little ship was about the size of the Terenure bus. It was eighty-six tons in weight or capacity, gross or net. Again I leave it to the experts.

We sailed with a mixed crew. Some had been on a boat before, and more hadn't. I was betwixt and between. I did many's the trip on the *Larssen* and the *Royal Iris** as a bona-fide traveller, but had never actually rounded the Horn, or stifled me mainbrace or anything of that nature.

The real sailors were the Skipper, the mate, and the fireman. The rest of the company were merchant adventurers along with the owner, and I was a merchant adventurer's labourer, so to speak.

The real sailors slept forrad and we had accommodation aft, where, as Sammy Nixon said, villainy could be plotted in peace.

Sammy came aboard wearing rather tasty pinstriped kid gloves and a Windsor knot of some dimensions. His hat he wore on the Kildare side, even in bed, for he had not a rib between him and heaven.

He had come straight from a pub in Belgravia, flown to Collinstown*, and after a stop for refreshments in Grafton Street, or thereabouts, had come down by taxi to the North Wall, where he had her tied up.

Sammy had never been on a boat of any description before, and till he had heard from Eddie, thought they'd been done away with like the trams.

Muscles Morgan, his china, was due on a later plane, and what old Muscles would say when he saw this lot Sammy did not know.

Muscles when he arrived dressed in the same uniform as Sammy, all eight stone of him, said: 'Corsalawk, e'n it? Lookah er, Namber One, cock,' which he repeated many times during our subsequent voyages, and Eddie, Sammy, Muscles, and I retired aft to drink rum, like sailors.

The sailors we left forrad, brewing their tea, darning their socks, winding the dockwatch and – with infinite skill – putting little ships into bottles. There would be no shortage of bottles. Before we thought of calling the Skipper we already had a couple of empties for the little ships to be put into them.

The Skipper fell to our level through drinking, gambling and sniffing. Just common sniffing. I am not unacquainted with the national catarrh but he was a most hangdog-looking man, with a sad puppy's face pleading for a friendship or, at least tolerance, and his shape and make was that of a Charles Atlas in reverse. And the whole world of ineffectual weakness was in that sniff.

147

Eddie picked him up in the West End and brought him over with the boat.

He sniffed nervously to me that he had never been in Ireland before though his family had a house in Mount Street and, if I possibly thought, if it would not, sniff, be too much, sniff, trouble, could I, would I not, presuming on our short acquaintance, tell him how to get there? His father was born in it.

Better than that. I would bring him to it. And did, after a couple of stops at other points of interest on the way. And he cried and sniffed and when I stood him with his back to Holles Street Hospital he looked up along Fitzwilliam Square and Fitzwilliam Place, lit by the sun on the mountains behind the long range of golden Georgian brick, and wept again and said there was not the like of it anywhere else.

So I got Eddie to call him down, and he sat in a corner and apologetically lowered an imperial pint of rum and hot orange. I think he took a subsidiary couple of rozziners to make up for the orange.

For if it's a thing I go in for in a human being it's weakness. I'm a divil for it. I thought of the Katherine Mansfield short story, where the daughters of the late colonel are afraid of the old chap, two days after his funeral, leaping out of the linen press on top of them, and one of them cries: 'Let's be weak, oh, please, let us be weak.'

He even sniffed an apology to Muscles and Sammy for their sea-sickness the first two days out while they lay in their death agonies and shuddered from the cup of rum he would minister unto them.

He lowered it himself and weakly took himself up on deck to look for the Saltees. We had a reason for going to France before the Six-Counties manifest would be of use to us.

When we came back for our turnips, the final arrangements had to be made with what I will call the Turnip Board, and we marched up the main street of a northern port on Armistice Day.

Eddie went into a shop and came out with two big poppies. I shook my head.

'No bottle?' said I, in his native language.

'None of this old mallarkey,' said he, 'there's a reason why I must get a cargo of turnips off these geezers.'

'That's not what I mean. They won't fancy poppies.'

'This is "Northern Ireland", 'nt it? They're for the King and Queen and all that lark, 'nt they?'

'Not here. This is "*southern* Northern Ireland".'

Eddie sighed. 'Only a nicker wasted,' and dropped his two ten-shilling poppies in the gutter. 'I get on. Mostly R.Cs. here, eh?'

We met the chairman of the Turnip Board in a hotel and Eddie shook him by the hand.

'I think it's an 'orrible shame the way these Protestants treat you 'ere, Mr. MacConvery.'

Mr. MacConvery's plum face turned blue and his stomach went in and out at a hell of a lick.

'The cheek of you,' he croaked; 'my old friend,' he indicated a little man like an undertaker's clerk sitting nearby, 'Mr. Macanaspie, respected member of the Presbyterian community, vice-chairman of the Turnip Board, we have it one year, they the next, chair and vice, turn an' turn about . . . I . . . '

His indignation collapsed for the want of breath and I got a chance to explain that it was a joke and it gave Eddie a chance to tell how he'd taken a prize in the Band of Hope himself.

And in the heel of the hunt we got the turnips and some months later in the bar of the Latin Quarter, as us old sea-dogs hove to in there, Eddie remarked that Partition was strategically useful.

Toronto Spinster Frowned

Myself and Winston Churchill were once upon a time in the same organisation; he as an Elder Brother of Trinity House and I as a painter for the Irish Lights. His position is more decorative than functional. I painted striped lighthouses, banded lighthouses and spotted lighthouses.

On the way down from Laganbank Road to Donaghadee, a schoolboy sitting beside me in the bus pointed out Stormont on one side of the road and remarked that Purdysburn Mental Hospital was further down on the opposite side.

I laughed in my rich southern brogue, low but musical, and an acid-faced lady in the seat in front called the schoolboy to order. When the seat beside her was vacant she called your man over to it and, glaring at me, breathed fiercely in his ear and he answered, 'Yes, auntie,' and 'No, auntie,' and sat staring straight in front of him for the rest of the journey.

It appeared that she didn't like 'Southerners'. I had not encountered this kind of carry-on before and it made me feel important and tragic, like the dust-jacket of a Peadar O'Donnell novel in the big block letters of the 'thirties.

By the same token, I wondered how Ireland lost

one of the cardinal points of the compass. We have songs, sneers, jeers and cheers for the Men of the West, the gallant South, the North Began and the North Held On, God Bless the Northern Land, and all to that effect, but damn the ha'porth about the East, except where Micheál Óg Ó Longáin gives us old Orientals a leg-up in a song about Ninety-Eight:

'Mo ghreidhn iad, na Laighnigh,
A d'adhain an tine bheo . . . '*

Máire MacEntee has a blood-rising translation of it but even at that it's in praise of the province – not a mention of our geographical direction nor a line for the Men of the East.

When someone calls me a 'Southerner' I feel like Old Black Joe.

'What part of the South do you come from, Rastus?'

'Ah sho' don' know, massah. It was dark when Ah left.'

When I heard her speak to the boy at the end of the journey I was surprised to notice that she had an American accent. In the bar that night I remarked on this to the fishermen I was with.

'Och aye,' says Old Andy, 'that'll be Miss Mackenzie. She's from Toronto, and she's in some Ulster Society over there to save us from yous. She can't bear the sight of a southern man and it's very dacent of her seein' as she was never in the country before in her life.' And to cheer me up, 'Of course, yous have a crowd in America too that goes round blackguarding us?'

In the morning I had to rewrite the notice on the lighthouse: 'Permission to view this lighthouse must be obtained from the Secretary, Commissioners for

151

Irish Lights, Westmoreland Street, Dublin.'

Only a portion of the old sign showed through the fresh paint but enough to let Miss MacKenzie know that an Ulster lighthouse had some connection with the rebels.

She was amongst a crowd of holiday-makers out for an after-breakfast stroll and breathed fury as I rewrote the sign on a surface previously coated with raw linseed oil: 'Permission to view this lighthouse must be obtained from Éamon de Valera, Leinster House, Dublin.'

I thought Miss Mackenzie would explode. She fulminated in the crowd but the people that go to Donaghadee in the summer have a deal to bother them, fishing young Sammy out of the harbour and trying to save Wee Bella from death by ice-creamitis. They gazed with mild interest after her as she dashed up to the Harbour Office.

By the time she got back, of course, I had the board rubbed dry and the official legend rewritten. She put her hand to her head and searched, distracted, for the offending words.

The harbour official looked at her and muttered something about the heat and ould ones going round in their bare heads. With innocent diligence I went on with my work.

Glossary

acushla: (Irish, a chuisle) my pulse, an affectionate term (128)
alanna: (Irish, a leanbh) child, an affectionate term (56)
a mhic: (Irish) son, an affectionate phrase (17)
a stór: (Irish) darling, my dear (71)
Aughrim: in Co. Galway, site of the last decisive battle in Irish history, fought on Sunday, 12 July 1691 (41)
'B' Specials: Civilian Protestant police force attached to the Royal Ulster Constabulary (116)
Blueshirts: Irish Fascist organisation (83)
breathnaigh isteach sna súile orm, a Ghráinne: (Irish) look into my eyes, Gráinne (102)
bunce in half a bar: (Dublin slang) put in sixpence, to pool resources (23)
burgoo: oatmeal porridge (16)
cailín: (Irish) a girl (63)
cawbogues: (Irish, cabhóg) cowards (116)
céilí: (Irish) friendly call, visit. Social evening. Irish music and dancing session (81)
cereal 's bainne: cereal and (Irish) milk (116)
chisellers: (Dublin slang) children (83)
clann: (Irish) family, clan (63)
Clann na nGael: (Irish) American Irish Republican group (75)
Collinstown: former name for Dublin Airport (147)
Croker: Croke Park, the Gaelic Athletic Association's main stadium (105)
do chum glóire Dé agus onóra na hÉireann: (Irish) for the glory of God and the honour of Ireland (132)
Michael Dwyer: 1771 – 1826, Insurgent leader (110)
Éire go bráth: (Irish) Ireland forever (59)
Éist, a chuid den tsaol. Is iad na tonntracha a chanfas amhrán ár

153

bpósta dúinn anocht . . . : (Irish) Listen, my love. The waves
   will sing our marriage song tonight . . . (101)
Feis Átha Cliath: Dublin festival (99)
Fianna: Fianna Éireann, national insurrectionary scout body
   (101)
Fianna Fáil: one of the two main political parties (61)
Fifteen Acres: area of playing fields in the Phoenix Park Dublin
   (109)
Fish Coyle: Feis cheoil, musical festival with competition (119)
flahool: (Irish, flaithiúil) generous, lavish, munificent (56)
G.N.R.: Great Northern Railway (141)
G.S.R.: Great Southern Railway (17)
gas: (Dublin slang) fun (54)
get: (Dublin slang) a wretch, a rogue (81)
go raibh míle maith agat, a Bhreandáin: (Irish) A thousand
   thanks, Brendan (80)
grá: (Irish) a liking or love for (32)
Grangegorman: a Dublin mental hospital (43)
gurrier: (Dublin derogatory slang) delinquent, corner-boy (96)
hard chaw: (Dublin slang) a tough person (55)
Haydock Park: English racetrack (143)
I.R.B.: Irish Republican Brotherhood (138)
*Is é rud atá ráite nár éirigh an cás leo, Ach an bás, ba é sin an
   t-aon rud bhí i ndán dóibh. Ach ba bheag leo an bás, agus Éire
   ina náisiún:* (Irish) The thing that's said about them is that
   their cause did not succeed, death was the only thing fated for
   them but death was a little thing to them if Ireland was a
   nation. (144)
jackeen: rural Irish nickname for Dubliner (81)
Jacks: the lavatory (86)
Larssen and Royal Iris: Dublin Bay paddle-steamers (146)
lights: animal lungs used as cat- and dogfood (16)
loy: spade (117)
maith go leor: (Irish) good enough (136)
the make in, fat, pontoon, ha'penny rummy: all games of cards
   except the 'make in', which is a street game played with a half-
   penny (a make) (105, 123)
mallarkey: (Dublin slang) messing, fooling around (99)
mangy: (Dublin slang) mean, selfish (109)
Milesians: one of the tribes cited in the Book of Invasions (145)

mo ghreidhn iad, na Laighnigh, a d'adhain an tine bheo: (Irish)
Hurray for the men of Leinster who kindled the living fire
(i.e. Insurrection) (151)

Monto: from Montgomery Street, Red light district of Dublin,
unfortunately demolished (18)

North William Gaeltacht: Irish speaking school in North William
Street, Dublin (124)

oíche mhaith duit: (Irish) Goodnight (87)

paicéad cáise agus punt crackers: (Irish) a packet of cheese and a
pound of (crackers) (116)

Parbleu, cad is fiú botún, thall is abhus: (Irish) Parbleu, what's a
few mistakes here and there (102)

Peeler: policeman. Sir Robert Peel (1788–1850) founder of Irish
Constabulary (114)

R.I.C.: Royal Irish Constabulary (136)

readies: (Dublin slang) money (57)

retrate: 'retreat', the lavatory (77)

Rising: Easter, 1916 (138)

Roto: The Rotunda, a Dublin maternity hospital (19)

rozziner: first drink (putting resin on the bow before playing)
(20)

saighdiúir eile Éireannach: (Irish) another Irish soldier (102)

scoil: (Irish) school (37)

scoraíocht: (Irish) an evening pastime or social evening (138)

Sea: (Irish) yes (103)

Séan T.: O'Kelly, former President of Ireland. (108)

Séimhiús and síneadh fadas: Irish grammatical accents (143)

Shinners (Sinn Féiners): members of Sinn Féin (111)

Sinn Féin: (Irish) we ourselves, a Nationalist Party (139)

skilly: prison food (28)

sláinte agus saol agaibh: (Irish) health and long life to you (76)

súgach: (Irish) cheerful, happy, mellow (84)

Tans: The Black and Tans. An armed auxiliary force sent by the
British government to Ireland in 1920 to suppress revolutionary activity (17)

Tír na nÓg: mythical land of eternal youth (128)

Toimeach Luimnigh: The Thunder of Limerick. Should this be
Turnamh Luimnigh (The Fall of Limerick)? (99)

Tóstal: (Irish) Pageant, National Festival which petered out.
(110)

Tuatha Dé Danann/Firbolgs: early races of Irish tradition (145)
uisce, an ea?: (Irish) water, is it? (99)
uisce, a Fhinn, tabhair deoch uisce chugam: (Irish) water, Finn,
   give me a drink of water (102)
Waxies' Dargle: celebrated annual holiday and outing of the
   Dublin cobblers (118)

Other Books from The O'Brien Press

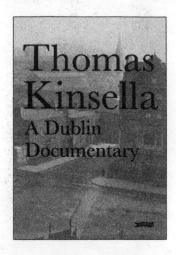

A DUBLIN DOCUMENTARY
Thomas Kinsella

A beautiful collection of poems, reminiscences and stunning photography brings Thomas Kinsella's Dublin to life. Here, Kinsella's poems are shaped around personal recollections of the places and people closest to his heart. We are offered an insight as to what inspired him to write these poems and the result is a deeply personal part-memoir, part-poetry collection that will be treasured by readers of Kinsella for years to come.

'An illuminating commentary'
THE IRISH TIMES

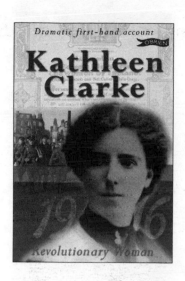

KATHLEEN CLARKE
Revolutionary Woman
Kathleen Clarke

Wife, mother, revolutionary, politician, Lord Mayor and widow Kathleen Clarke tells the inside story of 1916, which she helped to plan alongside her husband, Tom Clarke. She witnessed drama, injustice, insurrection, camaraderie and suffering. Kathleen Clarke tells, in her own words, the aftermath of her husband's and only brother, Ned Daly's, executions. She was imprisoned in Holloway Jail with Countess Markievicz and Maud Gonne MacBride; smuggled gold for Michael Collins and visited the dying Harry Boland. Later she became a Dáil deputy, a senator and the first woman Lord Mayor of Dublin, 1939.
'A remarkable work of enormous historical value' RTÉ

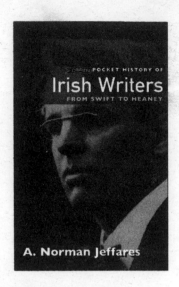

O'BRIEN POCKET HISTORY OF IRISH WRITERS
A. Norman Jeffares

This concise guide traces the long list of Irish writers, from Swift to the end of the twentieth century – Synge, O'Casey, Beckett, Joyce, Julia O'Faolain, Paul Durcan, Kate O'Brien, Roddy Doyle, Seamus Heaney ...